To ⋀

LONG SKIS//SHORT STORIES

enjoy !

Nov 2002

By the same author

Novels:

Winter Carnival (Queen)
A Farewell to Skiing
Under the Batholith

Still to come:

Show-ers
Mountains in the Stream
Long Skis//Short Stories Vol II

These can be found on *www.diadembooks.com*

LONG SKIS//SHORT STORIES

by Kurt Larson

Writers Club Press

San Jose New York Lincoln Shanghai

Long Skis//Short Stories

Writers Club Press
an imprint of iUniverse, Inc.

For information address:
iUniverse, Inc.
5220 S. 16th St., Suite 200
Lincoln, NE 68512
www.iuniverse.com

ISBN: 0-595-23618-9

Printed in the United States of America

For my brother Frank, who missed some great skiing adventures.

Contents

Foreword

Alpine Skiing has been a great way for me to see new places and make new friends. There's nothing better than being in the mountains, enjoying the solitude and getting away from the pressures of everyday life. Well, maybe one thing is better and skiing satisfies that, too. I've managed to meet some amazing women out on the slopes. It is also a good way to stay in shape and stay out of the bar. Then again, there's no better reason for going to the bar than after a hard day's skiing.

Skiing is a lifetime sport. You'll see that right away when you read this volume of *Long Skis//Short Stories*. I've recreated a few of my own experiences into a fictional format to give you a taste of what a wonderful adventure it is. I know you'll enjoy these short stories and hope they bring back fond memories of your own skiing adventures. If you don't ski, read this book and you might find you'll need to start. And wait—I've a few more stories I'd like to share with you soon.

Kurt Larson
Kingairloch, Scotland
July 2002

Costumes and Balloons

.

*L*ars and Judy ran up the stairs from the basement of Mt Hope Church. Sunday School was over and they were not going to church as usual afterwards. They were both going to go skiing instead. It was late March and the last day of the season out at the Ski Park. They were excited about the costume contest and wanted to get there on time.

At the top of the stairs they saw Pastor Bayer talking to the ushers and greeting the congregation. The Pastor looked tall and ominous in his white robes. One of the ushers in a bad-fitting brown suit put a finger to his lips as he saw the youngsters dashing up the stairs, Judy's pigtails swishing and both of them giggling away. They walked past the three men and out through the open double doors of the church entrance. Lars and Judy walked quietly on the clean concrete leading away from the entrance. The Pastor turned around to look at them. But before he could ask what they were doing and why they were not coming into church, the two children began to run to the car waiting for them.

White smoke was coming from the exhaust of the black Buick station wagon. When Lars and Judy opened the back door and piled in, still giggling, Judy's mom put down the Sunday edition of the *Detroit Free Press* she was reading. She was looking at the section with the spring women's fashions. The rest of the paper was on the back seat and Lars looked at the headline when he sat down. There were pictures and a story about plans for the astronauts to circle the moon for the first time.

Lars was sure there would be a similar article in the Sunday edition of the *Bay City Times*, which he'd read as soon as he got home from skiing today. Mrs Spencer would be sure to ask about it in school on Monday. That would be after 'show and tell,' always the first thing after a weekend. Both Lars and Judy hoped they would be telling about the prizes they hoped to win in the costume contest on the last day of skiing at Bear Mountain.

Judy's mom turned around and looked at the two of them. She gave them a big smile.

"So how was Sunday school then?" she asked.

"Same as always, mom. Can we go now?" Her daughter scrambled to look over at the things stored behind their seat in the back of the car.

"Not so fast, Judy. Did you learn anything new today?" her mother asked, just as she did every day.

"No mom. Let's go before the Pastor comes after us."

"Lars, how about you, or did the cat get your tongue?"

"Oh, it was fine, Mrs Binns. We learned about Jesus turning the water into wine. We also did a few songs and prayers asking us to be forgiven and forgive…"

"Lars!" Judy interrupted him with an elbow to his ribs and a giggle. "We'll never get to the hill if you keep talkin'." She turned to her mother. "C'mon, mom!" she pleaded.

"All right, all right," Mrs Binns finally gave in. "Hold your horses."

She put the column mounted gear selector into reverse. As she backed out her glance into the rear view mirror caught the intense blue eyes of that Svensson boy. He always had something to say, well beyond his age. His mentioning the wine reminded her that they were all out of booze after last night.

They were soon driving along M-72, just having crossed the six lines of bumpy railroad tracks on the outskirts of Grayrock. The studded snow tires on the Buick began to hum on the dry pavement once the car picked up speed. Mrs Binns looked at her watch. By the time she got the kids to the hill and back to town it would be mid-day. Glen's Market would be open and one could buy booze on a Sunday after 12 noon in Michigan. She listened to the hum of the tires and made a mental note to chase after that husband to arrange to have the snow tires changed before he went off to Saginaw on Wednesday. Winter certainly seemed to be over and with the sun shining like it was today the last of the snow would be gone real soon. She couldn't wait for the golf course to open. Her pals were just talking about it last night when they were over for a drink. As usual, they stayed too long.

All she had to do was the driving. That was it. She didn't feel bad about missing out on the plans some of the girls had made for today. They were all going out to the hill to meet up for a drink and see the kids in their costumes. They might be there by now. She drank enough last night and didn't need another excuse. Getting some groceries and some liquor would be a good thing and maybe she'd have some time to relax this afternoon before going back out to pick up Judy. *Yeah, that would be nice—to relax for a change,* she thought with a sigh. As the car crossed the bridge over the backwaters of the AuSable River she began to hum that song by Ike and Tina Turner, the one about rolling on the river and leaving a good job in the city.

When they veered off the highway and onto Military Road she told the kids they could start getting ready. That was the deal—no climbing around until they were in Karen Woods and on the road to the hill. Judy was quick to climb over the seat and hand Lars the two brown paper sacks embossed with Glen's green insignia. Then she handed over the ski boots—first her nice new Heneke buckle boots, then the lace-up ones that Lars used. Lars had told everybody he was going to get boots just like those for next season, but in a different color. That was even if he had to save all his money from shoe shining at Camp Grayrock over the summer.

They dressed into the costumes as the Buick rolled along, helping each other. Mrs. Bins would glance back occasionally to see if they were doing it right. The best thing about this whole costume lark was that she didn't have to do anything. Mrs Svensson had worked away and made those outfits from scratch on her sewing machine. Well, maybe she had used a pattern, but probably would have to change it to get it to fit over their clothes. And she had even come around to see Judy in their house on Michigan Avenue for the fittings. Probably nosey and wanting to see how they'd fixed the place up.

She drove down that old road now replaced by the big highway. Once past the subdivision they were onto the military reserve, nothing but scrubby jack pines until they approached the ski park. Things were beginning to happen out at the hill—the sewage treatment works which they passed, the big wide road with the flagpoles on either side going into the park, and the new hotel with its two bars, restaurant and swimming pool. But the one thing that hadn't changed was the tiny short hill now in front of them with the small day lodge at the foot of it. There were bald patches appearing along the top and puddles of water at the bottom where she parked the car. There were a few people out skiing. She recognized a few faces and gave a friendly wave and then heard Judy pleading from the back.

"Please, mommy, help me with my mask."

"I'll help you Judy," Lars perked up from where he was bent over tying his ski boot laces.

"No, I want mommy to do it. You messed up my hair the last time. Put your own mask on."

"Come around to my door then, honey," Mrs Binns announced, casting a glance in the rear view mirror to look at the Svensson boy begin to pull the blue cloth mask over his mop of stunning blond hair. Soon intense blue eyes peered through the slits in the mask. That boy is going to break some hearts one day, she thought to herself. Just like his father. She thought how he looked this morning, bringing little Lars to their big house on Michigan in that old pickup truck—straight off the farm, full of excitement about being in town for church and then skiing.

"Well, come on mom, I'm ready!" Judy shouted at the car window.

Mrs Binns opened her car door. The outside air felt surprisingly warm, a breeze blowing and the parking lot's asphalt wet from the melting snow. She motioned to her daughter to move closer and took the yellow strand of ribbon from her hand and began to position it and tie it around the back of her head. Lars had stepped out of the car and was taking his skis over to the racks. Other skiers were looking at him in his costume as he walked back towards the car with a big smile on his face.

"At least you won't need coats today," she told her ten-year old while shifting her pigtails to make them look neat with the mask.

"That's good, isn't it mommy? But its gonna melt the snow."

"But it is the last day of the season, darling."

"I know, mom. Are you done yet?"

"Nearly. Doesn't Lars make a handsome looking Batman?"

"Oh yuck, mom. You probably want me to kiss him, too."

"Only if you want to. But I don't think that Robin is that sort of a friend to Batman."

"Certainly not this caped crusader, mom. Are you done now?"

"Yes I am. Let me have a look at you"

Mrs Binns smiled as she watched her daughter do a little twirl and stumble about in her ski boots. She had to admit the costume looked great. The Svensson boy came over to stand beside her. They looked wonderful and she cast a thought to what they might look like together in ten years' time.

"A couple of cute caped crusaders if I ever saw them," she announced.

"C'mon Lars, lets go get our tickets and my skis from the locker," Judy replied and spun on her heel to walk towards the lodge.

"Thanks for taking us out here, Mrs Binns," Lars said, standing there looking at the woman who looked so different without her hair all done up, and without all that makeup and lipstick on. She looked older today. Usually she looked like a movie star.

She gave him a smile and looked at the little boy obviously proud with himself in the Batman costume, old battered skis with cable bindings and bamboo ski poles in his hands, seeing again those lovely blue eyes just looking at her through that mask.

"Don't mention it, Lars. Now you and Judy go have fun today. Oh, here's a coupla dollars." She reached down into the ashtray. "Buy Judy and yourself somethin' later." She handed Lars the notes, just wanting to see the expression on his face before she left him."

"Gee thanks, Mrs. Binns!" Lars exclaimed as he took the money and attempted to put the notes into his trousers beneath the gray and blue costume. The skis and poles were getting jumbled up and Mrs Binns laughed and stood out of the car seat to help him. She pulled the costume down and then took the notes out of his hand and folded them again and stuffed them down into one of his front pockets. Finally she pulled his costume up and patted him on the butt.

"I'll look after Judy," Lars said quietly and stepped back from Mrs Binns, feeling all bashful now. Beneath that mask his face felt hot and was probably bright red.

"We'll be back at four. Would you like a lift home, Lars?"

"No. No thanks. I'll probably ski home today, ma'am"

"You're such a good boy. Now run along. That Judy won't wait long for you."

"Thanks Mrs Binns. Bye."

Lars watched her start the station wagon up and reverse out of the parking lot. She gave him a wave and blew him a kiss as she drove away. Lars was blushing again but he felt happy and proud. He walked around the lodge to put his skis in the racks and go pick up a lift ticket and find Judy. He didn't mind some of the other skiers looking at him in his costume. He could see there were other kids already out on the hill skiing in theirs.

As Mrs Binns drove off she noticed the cars parked along the circular drive that led past the Polyhedron Hotel entrance. Between the hotel and day lodge was the new swimming pool. And next to the swimming pool was the bar. She recognized several of the cars parked conveniently close to the bar door. For a moment she thought about stopping to go join them but then thought better of it. After all, she was trying to do better in her new life after moving back to Grayrock.

It was darker in the lodge and Lars saw Judy over by her family's ski locker. She was playing with the combination lock and he heard the familiar click-chunk sound as it opened. He didn't mind not having a locker at the hill as he lived so close and could ski home. If he ever needed to store anything he would use Judy's locker. He walked over towards Judy, his boots clomping on the concrete floor.

"Hey, guess what, Judy. Your mom gave me some money."

"That was my money—give it to me!" Judy shouted as she turned around with her skis and poles wrapped in her arms. The skis tumbled onto the concrete floor with a crash.

"It's mine now. She gave it to me."

"Svensson, you little thief!"

"Don't worry Robin, Batman will come to your rescue. We'll share it. Your mom said I should buy you something to eat later."

She did her usual frown and put her hands on her hips, looking so grown up in her costume and mask though the pigtails just didn't seem to go along with all of it.

"We'll share it then. Don't just stand there—help me out with this stuff. And don't call me Robin. My name's Judy."

"Not today"

"You really like to play, don't you Lars?"

"Yes, I do. Let's go crush crime out there in Gotham City."

"Help me with my skis then."

Lars bent over and picked up the new pair of Hart Hornets. Judy always seemed to get new skis every year, even before she moved away a few years ago and came back again this year. He was going to have to wait another year before he could save up enough for skis. The boots would have to come first. They were pinching his toes as he carried the skis out to the racks and set them next to his old wooden ones with the cable bindings. When he got new skis he'd get those Cubco bindings, just like Judy had. He turned around to tell that to Judy but she wasn't there. She must have gone to get a lift ticket. He went back inside the lodge.

Judy was standing at the counter where they did the rental skis and the lift tickets.

One of the girls who went to the high school was stapling her day ticket onto a new wire that had been pushed through the material of her costume top. The high school girl was bent right over the counter and two of the boys from the high school who worked with her were watching her trying to close the big staple gun. The stapler was tethered to the counter by a chain and the chain was tight. One boy came out from behind the counter and while they were all laughing he took the stapler from the girl and finished the job. Lars knew the boy was Gerry Klinsman, the captain of the ski team. Gerry lived out at the lake and used to ride the same bus as Lars and his brothers. But now Gerry had a car and he had seen him and the girl together in it many times.

"Hey Gerry, will you help me with mine, too?" Lars asked when he joined them.

"Sure, little Svensson, er... Batman!" he exclaimed back. Gerry was always friendly.

"Just be sure to sign the book," the girl said, now back behind the counter while trying to tuck her shirt back in. She pulled one of the thin cardboard tickets out of the drawer beneath the counter. Then she forced the date stamp onto the ticket with the big metal tool that always sounded so serious and official when it slammed down onto the counter. Lars reached for the spiral notebook and looked at the various signatures running down a column beneath today's date. He could tell who was out skiing at that moment by looking at the list. He signed his name beneath Judy's, trying to make it as neat as he could. He was glad he could do handwriting now, especially writing his name.

He took the ticket and one of the thin wires from the counter. He gently poked the wire through the material of his costume. Then he turned towards Gerry who was still holding the stapler. Gerry smiled at him and took the ticket. He folded it in half and then stapled it several times to secure it around the wire.

"There's another one for your collection, Lars."

"Yeah. Too bad I didn't have my jacket. We could have just stapled this with the others."

"Batman doesn't wear a jacket, does he?" Gerry teased.

"No, I 'spose not."

"How many days do you think you skied this year anyhow, Lars?"

"I dunno. Maybe a hundred, including the night skiing."

"Count up your tickets when you get home. I bet it's at least that. You've been out here as much as Larry and he thinks he did over a hundred."

"But he's bigger."

"So what? You keep on practicing and you'll be better. Whatever the number, you got your money's worth this year."

"What about you, Gerry?" Judy butted in to ask. "Did you get your money's worth?"

"Yeah, I'd say so. In more ways than one." He smiled at Judy and then turned to look at the girl who smiled back at him.

One of the local doctors and his wife who were also members came strolling along to sign the book and get their tickets.

"You kids run along now," Gerry said. "We'll see you out on the hill."

"You're coming skiing later?" Lars asked and didn't wait for a reply. "That's great!"

"Just as soon as I get the rental stuff put away. I wouldn't want to miss the costume judging. Larry's out there already. He and Jane think they're gonna win."

"No way!" Judy exclaimed. "We're gonna win."

"What time is the judging?" Lars asked.

Gerry looked at his watch. "Oh, round about three I'd say, depending on what time they get themselves together over at the Poly."

"Well, at least we can get some runs in."

"That's the spirit! We'll announce it on the PA. That reminds me. Why don't you put on that Doors album, Patti? Let's liven this place up."

"Hey, Gerry, could we get some tickets?" The doctor asked. He lived near the Klinsmans out at the lake.

"Don't they look cute?" The doctor's wife said. "Isn't that the Svensson boy from the farm on Military?"

"Hi Mrs Beaton," Lars replied. "We're just going skiing now."

"And you must be Judy? Nice to see you back here. Your mother and I used to…"

"C'mon Lars, let's get on the hill—I want to ski," Judy interrupted and turned her back on the people inside the lodge.

Lars shrugged his shoulders at the doctor and the doctor's wife and Gerry and the girl and boy behind the counter and followed her outside.

Judy already had her skis on as Lars came out of the Lodge. Those Cubco bindings she had sure were easy, he thought. He took his skis off the rack and set them on the snow. He stepped into the toe piece and then had to jiggle the plastic-covered steel cable until it went around the ridge on the heel of his boot. He tightened the cable by pushing the lever down ahead of the toe piece. Then he had to wrap the safety strap around the boot and secured it. He looked over at Judy who was just finishing clipping each of her short safety straps to a buckle on each boot. He wasn't too far behind her and he worked quickly to put the other ski on. He grabbed his bamboo poles and Batman and Robin were ready to go skiing.

"Should we go up number one?" Judy asked, already setting off in the direction of the rope tow. That was the closest lift to the lodge and there was no line but he could tell it was running as the return pulley was spinning. He looked at the T-bar and there was a short line forming there, several of his friends in costumes. If they took the rope tow they'd beat them to the top. He pushed on after Judy and saw why so few people were using the rope tow to the top of Bear Mountain. There was a big puddle of water lying over the snow in the loading area. But it was still possible to go around the water and get on the tow as a tiny causeway of snow ran from the fenced-in pulley to the tracks directly beneath the rope. Lars skated past Judy as if to show her the way and they stopped at the loading point.

"Look at all that water!" Judy exclaimed.

"It's really melting, Judy," Lars replied, looking over towards the bunny slope through the leafless oak trees.

That tow wasn't even running as there was a huge pool of water at the bottom of the short slope. Past the bunny slope through a group of trees was the toboggan run and beyond that the military reserve in the woods. The Svensson's farm was through those woods bordering the reserve and Lars would have to ski through that this afternoon to get home.

"Well, are we going to go up?" Judy asked impatiently.

"Yeah. I was just looking at all the water. I'm gonna have to ski through that later."

"It'll be like water skiing, Lars. Think of it as fun."

"You might be right, Judy. Let's get up the hill. Go over to the bowl. That's where everybody is."

Judy stepped up ahead of Lars to reach for the thick yellow nylon rope that was spinning around the tail pulley and whizzing past them. As she tried to grip the rope it just slid through her hands and she lifted them up and looked over her shoulder at Lars.

"The rope's wet and I can't grip it with these gloves!"

"Let it slide under your armpit until you can hold on," he offered.

He never thought the costume gloves his mom had made would be no good for the rope tow. Judy did as she was instructed and tried to let the rope slide between her arm and chest until she was gripping enough to pull away and she gently grasped the rope with her hands and was riding up the tow. He watched her shift her hands to the position they were instructed to use, right arm in front, left one behind the back grasping the rope, ski poles strapped onto the left hand. He stepped up to do the same exercise.

Soon he was traveling up behind Judy. She was right—the rope was wet but not too bad. The moisture had already gone through the thin blue cloth and his hands stung a little from the rope sliding through his hands until he grasped it and set off. But if Judy could do it, then so could he. That was the price he had to pay for being Batman for a day, this last day of skiing at Bear Mountain.

Riding up, he thought for a minute about the price his parents had to pay to allow his brothers and sisters to go skiing. He felt lucky that they had bought a family membership this year—ninety dollars for all of them instead of $18 per person. It seemed like a lot to Lars when his mom told him back at Thanksgiving. He had given his mom a hug then and wasn't ashamed about doing that. He didn't give her a hug for making the costumes but maybe he would when he got home, hopefully with a prize to show her.

When they came to the first offloading point Lars hoped that Judy would follow his plan and keep going. The next rope ran along the ridge past the toboggan house and up to the T-bar summit. It was set at a dogleg to the first tow and if you did it right and nobody was in the way you could just let your speed carry you onto the tow—none of that slipping of the rope through your hands, just the fun of speed on skis and grasping the next rope and remembering to keep going. Judy had tried to do that but she had slowed down. There was a thin film of water lying across the flat landing point and she had gone through it. He managed to dodge around the water and his speed brought him right behind Judy. Luckily she had grasped the rope and was moving away with Lars right behind her. She turned her head and gave him a smile, then looked forward as there were bumps in the towpath. This was a shorter tow and he could see the top where the rope and the T-bar met. He could also see the rust-colored jacket of a ski patrolman up there looking in his direction.

Lars loosened his grip on the rope and let some slide through his hands. It was probably too late. He'd been spotted by the ski patrol who just stood there glaring at Lars as he came off the tow just behind Judy. There was only one thing to do—get it over with.

"Haven't you kids learned anything this year?" they were asked in a deep voice as they crossed through the path of the T-bar line and towards the top of the run everybody called the Bowl. Lars had made sure to stop and look both ways before crossing the T-bar path but it probably didn't matter.

"Hey, I looked both ways," Judy pleaded, then turned and looked at Lars.

"My fault, Mr Schumacher," Lars said, looking straight at him.

"I take it that's our Mr. Svensson behind the Batman mask. Can you see all right through that mask, young man?"

"Yessir, I can see fine."

"Then use your eyes next time and give the young lady a bit of space on the rope."

"Guess I went a bit too fast off the number one, sir. I don't think we'll be taking the rope again today." Lars looked at Judy. She nodded her head in agreement.

"Well, remember that for next year, Svensson."

"Yessir."

"And don't try to water ski through the big puddle at the bottom of the Bowl. It's deeper than it looks. I don't know what your parents would say if you came home all wet in those nice costumes."

"I don't think they'd care," Judy replied smartly, thinking that the scolding was over with now.

"That's the point." Mr Schumaker said and shook his head and skied off to the crest of the hill.

Judy turned to Lars and began to giggle. He just looked at her in the costume with the yellow mask and her brown pigtails sticking out.

"What's so funny?" he asked.

"Mr Schumacher. Dad always said he couldn't be a policeman so this must be the next best thing."

"Judy, why are you so rude to everybody?"

"Because I can get away with it—I'm Judy Binns," she answered in that smart sounding tone. Before he could say anything else she looked at two other kids riding up on the T-bar. "Hey! It's Larry and Jane! They're cowboys and Indians. Hi Jane!"

Lars looked at the two of them coming up the T-bar together and when they were on the flat at the top he watched them release it. The hydraulic cylinder of the bar hissed as it retracted and they began to ski over towards Lars and Judy. Both of them were in eighth grade and always seemed older. Today, with their costumes on, they all looked the same age. Their costumes looked good and Lars wondered if he and Judy would be able to beat them in the judging. For now they would be friendly and try to ski together until the contest started. Lars wanted to ski now.

"You guys look great!" Jane exclaimed as she skied over to the younger pair.

"Not bad, Svensson, " Larry stated, looking him over. "Check out my gun."

"Cool, Larry," Lars replied. "Lemme see it."

"Judy, that costume is going to win for sure," Jane asked. "Where did you get it?"

"Lars' mom made it. She made his too."

"I didn't think that your mom would have done that."

"I bet your mom didn't make yours either," Judy replied smugly, then added, "I thought you said she was coming skiing?"

"She's down at the Poly right now, smarty pants. She stayed there last night, to get things ready if you wanna know. Larry's big brother brought us all here."

Lars was looking at the toy gun that Larry had pulled out of the leather holster. It all looked so real. He had leather riding chaps on and a sheepskin vest along with the cowboy hat his big brother had brought back from Colorado. But while he looked at Larry's gear he listened to Jane and knew there was trouble. Jane and Judy were cousins. Jane's dad didn't live with her mom any more. And it seemed strange that she was staying at the Poly just for the costume contest. The costume contest was a big thing to Lars but he didn't think it was that big a thing for grown-ups.

"Them girls can stay there yakking," Larry announced as he put the gun back in the holster.

"Yeah, let's get some runs in," Lars replied.

"Follow me then," Larry said and took off over the crest.

Lars took one look over at Judy and Jane. Beneath her headdress Jane looked like Judy's mom and even looked prettier with her makeup on, her cheeks nice and red to make her look like an Indian.

Jane smiled at Lars with those eyelashes so big and dark while she kept talking to Judy. He felt himself beginning to blush again and he decided to set off down the hill after Larry. He had to dodge the patches of dirt now appearing right at the top but that was easy to do.

Once he made a turn or two everything was fine. He felt pretty good now, wearing his Batman costume. It was much better than anything he wore at Halloween—even better than that now because he was skiing in his costume. The wind in his face felt good, rushing between the slits in his mask. The small fins that his mom had sewn into the gloves flapped up and down in the breeze he was making for himself by going fast over the snow.

The snow felt funny. It was almost like tiny ball bearings beneath his skis. But once he got used to it he found this corn snow was soft enough and easy to turn on—not at all like the artificial snow made by those mean looking men. It would turn to ice and all you did was slide on it. This stuff you could grip on and it felt good so he kept making turns but still went fast so that he could catch up to Larry. By the time he was just behind Larry they were skiing side by side, coming down the last pitch over the edge of the bowl and down to the lift line.

Down at the bottom was that big puddle of water, just as Mr Schumaker had said. Lars was tempted to have a go and see if he could ski right through it but instead followed Larry and went around it, keeping up enough speed to carry himself across the flat ground and into the lift line. They both stopped and looked up the hill. Some of the other skiers in the lift line looked at them in their costumes.

"There's Judy and Jane," Larry said and everybody seemed to turn their heads and look up the hill. The T-bars were clattering as they went around the flywheel and people were boarding the lift and making their way back up the hill. Lars watched the girls making lazy turns and waited for the last people to board before he spoke to Larry.

"They look great, don't they Larry?"

"They sure do."

"I mean Jane, she looks, well, really pretty."

"Yeah, she kinda overdid the makeup though."

"But you really like her, don't you."

"Yeah, I guess so."

"I hope I can like Judy one day."

"Whadda mean?"

"Well, I don't think she likes me, so I can't like her."

"Of course she likes you, Lars. She just needs time to get to know you."

"How much time does it take? I've been trying ever since she moved back here."

"I dunno. As long as it takes. I've been trying with Jane since before her mom and dad got in that fight. It seems easier now."

"You're lucky, Larry. Look at her. She's so pretty."

They were watching the two girls coming down the last bit of the hill now. Jane cut to her right to go around the water puddle. But Judy stopped turning and went straight, heading for the water with Lars and Larry standing on the other side of it waving their ski poles for her to stop or turn or do something. But she kept going straight at them. The only thing for Lars and Larry to do was move out of her way and watch as she approached the puddle. In she went, her skis at first skimming over the surface of the water. The water then began to spray up beneath her skis and she lost speed quickly and the skis began to sink below the surface of the water. She came to rest with the water level just below the tops of her new ski boots. Lars and Larry were laughing and Jane came over and joined them. They looked at Judy in her Robin outfit with her hands on her hips and a scowl on her face. She began to wade through the water until she made it to the edge where the others stood.

"Holy cow, Robin!" Larry exclaimed. "That's not water skiing!"

"It's not funny. And I'm the one who's supposed to say that. At least I'm not a chicken."

"At least I'm not wet," Lars added in response.

"If you want to know, these boots don't leak. Not like your crappy old ones."

"No need to be high and mighty, Judy," Jane said.

"*You* should talk—you and your mom always showing off, all those fancy dresses and makeup."

"Girls, girls!" Larry admonished. "We're here to ski and have fun. Let's get up the hill."

"Good idea, Larry," Lars said. "I'd like to get some runs in. It's the last day after all." He headed for the T-bar boarding spot.

They all skied together in the corn snow. It became slushier as the afternoon went on. They all kept looking for signs of people coming out of that Polyhedron Lodge and listening for an announcement that the judging was going to start. More kids had arrived in their costumes and everybody was skiing and shouting and having fun but still waiting for the contest to start. Lars was looking down at the door coming out of the bar by the swimming pool and he thought he saw somebody. Instead of watching where he was going he nearly ran into Judy and only prevented a collision by falling down quickly. It was the only time he would fall all day. The corn snow had a funny texture when he skidded on it, almost like coarse sandpaper.

Through the afternoon there was cheerful music playing on the loudspeaker. As they skied down the short run they could hear that song called *Sugar, Sugar* by the Archies. It was better than that weird sounding stuff about riders on storms and then that other group singing about white rabbits and pills that made you small. The girls were singing the words to that sugar song on the way up the lift. Everybody was having fun but they were all waiting for the costume judging to begin.

Waiting at the top of The Bowl, Lars could see Gerry and his girlfriend riding up the T-bar. He pointed them out to Larry who nodded and they both hoped that maybe now this costume judging could begin. Gerry stopped to talk to the two boys while his girlfriend tightened her new ski boots. She had those Henkes just like

Judy, just in a bigger size. Gerry told Lars he should be finishing his turns more by pushing his knees in and putting more weight on his downhill ski. He was always offering Lars advice and Lars was listening but also watching down at that Polyhedron for any signs of activity. Finally he saw what looked like other people in brightly colored costumes coming out. He also saw Judy and Jane skiing over towards the Polyhedron along with some of the other kids in their costumes.

"Look Larry, that must be the judges coming out now!" Lars exclaimed, interrupting Gerry's instruction.

"Hey Lars, you're right!" Larry replied. "And there's the girls heading over. We'd better get down there quick!"

"Let's bomb it!" Lars offered.

Gerry offered some more advice: "There's plenty of time, you guys. Don't waste a good run. It might be the last of the season."

His younger brother didn't pay much attention to that command. He just pulled his cowboy hat down tight and pulled the chinstrap in, then tucked his ski poles under his shoulders and set off down the fall line. He was away and going fast but nearly fell as he went over some of the moguls at the top of the run. Lars looked at Gerry who shrugged his shoulders. Gerry looked at his girlfriend who smiled back at the two of them. Some of the older people were staying out skiing but all of the young ones in costumes were gathering at the back door to that Polyhedron lodge.

"Please, Gerry," Lars asked.

"You can do what you want," Gerry said, adding, "But you'll never be a good skier if you don't work at it."

"Okay, Gerry—you're right," Lars said quickly. "I'm gonna ski down through the bumps and then let loose. I'll still catch Larry."

"Well, you'd better get going then," Gerry said.

Lars had already pointed his skis down into the fall line and was going fast. He decided he would make big turns and ride over the bumps and go as fast as he could. He looked ahead and picked his line to cut around the bumps. It felt good and he felt fast and everything whizzed past and soon he was catching up on Larry. He made good wide fast turns right down to the flat section about halfway down the slope and then bombed it, getting low into a tuck and carrying his speed and coming over the rise and then hit the slope at full speed. He could see the other kids down at the lodge and he wanted to have as much speed as possible coming up to it. The tiny wings on his gloves were flapping with the slipstream he made. He caught Larry and they went up the slope to the lodge door and came to a quick fast stop, spraying up the wet corn snow with everybody looking at them.

Some adults came out of the steel and glass double doors that were sort of an emergency exit from the back of the bar. They were laughing and shouting and stumbling around. They wore costumes, but not the type Lars or any of the other kids expected. And they carried drinks in their hands—most of them glasses of a red tomato juice liquid with a piece of celery stuck in it. Lars didn't know what to make of it at first but thought they were just adults going along with the costume party on the last day of skiing.

It was the balloons, mainly, that caught his attention. Four women had come out of the bar with nothing but balloons taped or pinned to their underwear. He could see bits of their underwear at times as a slight breeze blew the balloons about. The women all had white skin with Goosebumps sticking out on their arms and legs right down to the high heels they were wearing. He recognized one of the women as Jane's mom. He looked over at Jane who was standing with Judy and Larry just a few feet away. Jane's face was even brighter red, and when she glanced at Lars she buried her face in her hands.

One of the men tried to get everybody's attention. He was wearing a deer-hunting outfit—bright red wool shirt and black with red checker striped wool trousers. The wool billed hunting cap matched the trousers. The man's face was unshaven. Lars finally recognized him as the man from the TV station in Cadillac. He hosted an outdoors show every Wednesday night. Lars didn't really like the show because all it covered was fishing in the summer and snowmobiling in the winter, and just a little on deer hunting and nothing ever on skiing. Maybe he was going to change that now by being here for the last day of skiing at Bear Mountain.

He began to speak. He had a big cigar in his hand and took an occasional puff after having a sip of his drink and then that familiar deep voice got everybody's attention.

"Let's get this thing over with—these broads are getting cold," he said and the kids began to gather around and the women in their underwear with the balloons attached giggled. The other men who came out also in hunting gear sort of moved to one side and sipped their drinks.

"I'd like to thank you all for comin' out here today," the man continued. "I hope you kids are having a good time on your last day of skiing. We're havin' a great time, aren't we, ladies?" He leaned towards Jane's mom. She leaned away and he reached over with his cigar and popped one of the balloons. The other women laughed and Jane's mom tried to turn away from the crowd as more of her pink cotton underwear was showing with a balloon gone from her backside.

The man puffed on his cigar and looked at the kids and laughed to himself. Then he had another sip of his drink. "Jus' love that Tabasco," he muttered. The group of children watched in silence.

"Dontcha think these ladies look great?" he asked out. None of the kids replied.

"Think I'm gonna give them a prize—the only prize! First prize in this here costume judging!"

A few of the kids groaned and just looked at each other as the man walked over to the women. One of the other men had been holding a small cup beside his pot belly. Lars recognized him as the manager of the ski park. Everyone watched him scratch his unshaven face while he held a smoldering cigar.

A woman reluctantly stepped towards the manager of the ski park and he handed her the tiny brass cup and she bent over to pretend to kiss his unshaven face and the TV presenter was looking at her backside covered in the balloons. He stepped towards her and used the lit end of the cigar again to pop several balloons rapidly. All the adults laughed as the balloons popped and everyone could see the woman's black underwear. None of the children were laughing.

Lars turned around and saw Gerry coming down the hill, making those smooth, relaxed yet powerful turns as he approached and came to stop beside him. His girlfriend was not far behind and she slid down and stopped beside him and smiled at Lars.

"What's going on?" Gerry asked Lars.

"They've given the prize to those women with the balloons," Lars replied. "They haven't even bothered to look at us." He pointed one of his bamboo ski poles at the group of adults who were now laughing and drinking and standing together.

Gerry bent down and released the heelpieces on his Marker bindings. He left the new Rossingol Strato skis lying on the soft spring snow and stomped off towards the adults. Lars started to undo his safety straps and the cable bindings and he followed on after Gerry. By the time he got there Gerry and the TV presenter were in an argument. Some of the women with the balloons were heading back into the bar. Very few balloons were still left unexploded and Lars watched their backsides wiggling in various colors of underwear and balloons as they pranced back into the bar.

Jane's mom had gone over to speak to Jane and Judy. Lars watched while Jane stood there crying, wearing her costume while her mom stood next to her wearing the balloons and underwear, pleading with her and not making any sense. Jane's mother put her hands to her head in disgust and walked towards the bar door and went back inside. Judy started making her way back towards the T-bar.

Lars saw Gerry turn and walk away from the TV presenter. His face was red and he came up to Lars and spoke to him sternly.

"C'mon Svensson, let's go skiing. This is no place for you kids to be."

"Okay Gerry. I just want to say hello to that TV guy."

"He's an asshole. But suit yourself." Gerry kept on walking past, back towards the girls who were still huddled together.

Lars walked on towards the man who was now finishing his drink and cigar.

"Hey mister!" Lars cried out as the man was heading back inside.

"Yeah kid, whadda want?" the man answered back in a gruff voice, tossing the smouldering cigar end into a melting snowbank by the door.

"Those ladies. I don't think it was very nice, the way you treated them."

"That's none of your frigging business, kid. We were just having fun."

"Your fun wrecked our contest. It wasn't very funny to me."

"Hey kid, get lost. I've had enough of your lip." The man opened the door with the empty glass in his hand. Lars could hear music coming from the jukebox in the darkened bar. He shouted back over the noise and managed to get the man's attention.

"Hey mister! Your show sucks!"

The man took a step in Lars' direction as if to come after him but then must have thought better of it and walked back into the bar. Lars stood there looking at the dark glass windows surrounded by the metal frame of the bar door. He took a long moment to look at his reflection on the glass and thought the costume still looked good. Then he turned around and walked back towards his skis.

All of the other kids had left and he watched them pushing across the snow towards the T-bar in their costumes. He put his skis on, saying to himself he would never watch that *Michigan Sportsman* show again.

He skied across to the T-bar and went up and joined the others and they all skied together for the rest of the afternoon. He looked after Judy like he promised her mom and bought her a pop and a bag of potato chips when they finished skiing. They didn't talk about the adults and the balloons.

Just before Judy's mom arrived Judy asked if he wanted the costume back. Lars said no, she could keep it. When the black Buick rolled in front of the Lodge, he walked out with Judy and said hello to her mom and goodbye to Judy. When Judy's mom asked how the costume contest went they both said "Okay" quietly and Judy said she would tell her about it on the way home.

Lars skied home through the woods wearing his Batman costume. While he pushed himself along and dodged the water puddles on the last of the snow he thought about forgiveness and forgiving. When he got home dinner was waiting in the oven. After he finished dinner he read about the astronauts in the paper and wanted to talk about them in school on Monday.

Pro Race

*T*hey drove through freezing rain going north on I-75. It had just turned to wet snow, sticking to the windshield of the Ford Pinto. As Harry braked for the stop sign coming off the ramp at the Gaylord exit the car skidded right through the intersection. Not seeing any traffic he kept going, sliding the tail of the Pinto from right to left as he tried to steer his way under the expressway and towards Boyne City.

"It's pretty slick out there," Harry said to Kent sitting beside him.

"Don't worry, we'll make Svensson shovel if we get stuck," Kent chuckled and cast a glance towards the back seat, grinning through his braces. "Why do you think we brought him along anyhow?"

Lars Svensson sat forward in his seat. He pushed some unkempt blond hair away from his ears as if it would help him to hear. It wouldn't make much difference. The 8-track tape player was blaring out the hard driving rhythms of Bachman-Turner Overdrive and their hit, *Takin' Care of Business*.

"It's only about an hour to Boyne form here," Harry said, relaxing a little now that he had the car under control. He tapped the palms of his hands on the steering wheel as he drove through the slush, tinted brown from all the road salt. He flicked the wipers on to clear the wet snow off the windshield.

"They'll have the plows out on 31," Kent said. "Piece of cake."

Lars leaned even further forward so that they could hear him. "Do you think they'll cancel the race on account of the snow?" he asked.

"You're even more stupid than you look," was Kent's response. Harry glanced at Lars and was a bit more diplomatic, giving Lars a smile.

"I wouldn't worry. There's no way they'll cancel with all those big names there."

"Guess I'll shut up till we get there then," Lars said as he slumped back into the seat and looked out at the snow falling on the outskirts of Gaylord. They were passing farms full of Christmas trees planted along both sides of the road. All he could hear was the fuzzy noise mixed with the music coming from the speakers behind him.

This weekend saw the Pro Skiing circuit make a stop in Michigan on its way out west. Lars couldn't wait to see the racers he always read about in the skiing magazines but only saw once in awhile on TV. Today he was going to get to see them, up close. Members of the Grayrock High ski team had been invited by Boyne City's coach to be gatekeepers at the race. Lars was one of the first ones to volunteer.

He thought he was pretty good at gate keeping as he did it all the time. He wasn't eligible to race for the high school yet because he was only in eighth grade. He couldn't drive yet either so he had to ask Harry who lived near him out at Lake Margaret. Harry was a senior and a good racer. Kent was a junior and didn't like Lars. That was probably because Lars could already beat him in time trials at practice when he got the chance. Most of the time he spent gate keeping at practice and that's why he thought he was well qualified to come to the Pro Race.

Lars was what they called a 'manager.' It was a strange title. He was never told what it really meant. It was nothing like Mayo Smith who was Manager of the Detroit Tigers. Some of his friends that helped out with the high school football team were also called ' managers.' They didn't manage anything either. They just picked up equipment after autumn practice sessions and got to go to the away games with the team. Lars picked up the bamboo poles after practice, just like his friends picked up the dirty uniforms after a football game.

Lars wasn't sure about what a lot of things meant. Like when Harry and Kent were talking about their girlfriends before the car stereo drowned him in noise earlier in this car. He liked girls but wasn't sure if he wanted a girlfriend from what they were saying.

One thing he was sure about was that he wanted to be a ski racer. Back in fourth grade his teacher had the class write a paragraph about what they wanted to be when they grew up. They had to write the paragraph in half an hour and not make a single mistake. Lars began his paragraph with, 'I would like to be a Olympic ski racer like Jean Claude Killy or Billy Kidd.' He then went on to explain all about the practicing; the traveling; and the racing down mountains. He thought he'd done pretty well. Mrs Funk failed him because he used 'a' in front of 'Olympic' instead of 'an.' Making that mistake did not change his thinking.

Lars still couldn't believe that Killy and all the other pro racers were coming to Michigan for a stop on the their North American tour. It wasn't the Olympics, but that didn't matter. It was being sponsored by a cigarette company who said it was good for their 'Midwest Market' to call in at Boyne Mountain on their way from Vermont to Colorado. Lars didn't care what the reason was for the pro race coming to Michigan. It was enough that he was going to get a chance to see it.

The snow had stopped falling and the sky was clearing as they drove north on US 31. Lars sat in the back of that Pinto, scraping the ice off the windows and looking at the scenery, thinking about his chances to meet the racers today. The hills at Boyne came into view, parallel strips of white cut through the darker covering of leafless trees. Two strips of red ran down either side of a trail right in the middle of the complex. He knew what that was. He leaned forward and shouted over the noise of the stereo.

"Look! That must be the course! It's on Hemlock, there in the red!"

"No shit, Sherlock," Kent replied, the 'sh'-sound hissing through his braces.

"I can see the jumps, too. They look huge!"

"Listen Svensson, if I want any lip from you I'll scrap it off my zipper."

Lars didn't pay any attention to what Kent was saying and he didn't know what he meant by his remark anyhow. He just kept staring up at the course, itching to get out of the car and go have a look at it.

A fleet of pickup trucks mounted with snowplows were working as they pulled into the parking lot. The newly fallen snow was being cleared rapidly and the hill was getting ready for a big day. The parking lot was empty as they were early, just a few cars and vans parked in front of the lodge. Up beyond the lodge on the hill Lars could see people already out inspecting the course. They pulled up right in front of the lodge beside a van with big letters written on the side advertising a make of skis Lars had not heard of which had the shape of a hexagon as its logo. The van must have been there a few days based on the fresh snow lying on it.

Harry pulled the 8-track out of the player and the inside of the car went quiet. It was surprisingly stuffy inside the Pinto. Lars felt his ears ringing in the silence and he barely heard Harry say, "They've been here a few days, for sure. I saw them on the news last night." Lars had also seen the short report on Channel 9 after he had come home from skiing practice. They had carried out an interview with Jean-Claude Killy. He said he was looking forward to the race and trying to improve his place in the overall rankings, as he was a few points behind Spider Sabich. When asked about the $25,000 first place he replied with something in his French accent like, "Eeets not as important as ze points for ze overall title."

"You gonna sit there all day or what?" Kent shouted at him. He and Harry were already out of the car and around at the rear with the hatchback door open. Lars had been sitting there thinking about the

TV interview and trying to picture what the race would look like today. The sudden blast of cold air coming into the car shocked him.

"Yeah, Lars," Harry said. "We gotta be in the lodge for a gate-keeper's meeting at eight thirty. Better put your ski boots on now in case we gotta go straight out on the hill."

After loosely buckling up ski boots and grabbing jackets and hats and gloves, the three began walking towards the lodge. "We'll come back for the skis. I'll leave them locked up there in the ski rack," Harry said as they walked through nearly a foot of new snow on the path leading into the lodge. Nobody had been out yet to shovel it.

"They'll have to do a lot of slipping for that course. Must have set it last night," Kent said.

"I think they're already doing it," Lars replied, taking up the rear in the group but now hearing what they were saying in the clear morning air.

"You'll probably want to set the gs, if you think you're so smart, Svensson," Kent replied.

Lars didn't say anything. He knew Kent didn't like him and was showing it as usual. He also knew that they would be setting the gs tonight after the dual slalom today. He would not be coming tomorrow as he had to do the Sunday morning paper route of the *Bay City Times*. He had persuaded his older sister to do it for him today so that he could come to the race.

They walked into the lodge right beneath the big clock tower and saw a small sign directing them upstairs to the gatekeeper's meeting. Their ski boots clomped on the concrete steps as they made their way up and into the room. The place was already full of other high school racers who had turned out to gate keep. Lars recognized a few of the faces from races held at Bear Mountain near his home in Grayrock. He had only been to one away meet and that's where he had first seen Carol. She was sitting by herself towards the back of the room, looking confident just like she did on the hill. And she looked so fresh and pretty. Even better in Lars' mind was that she was a good racer, already Gaylord high's number one girl. She was a sophomore and that meant she was much older than Lars and would not pay much attention to him, so he took a seat in the back row of the room behind her. Kent took a seat beside her and started straight in on talking to her. Harry was still standing and talking to one of the racers from Harbor Springs. Everybody in the room seemed to be talking to somebody else except for Lars and the room was noisy. It suddenly went quiet when a tall man wearing an orange baseball cap with the words *Hanson* on it came into the room. He was carrying a box stuffed full of manila envelopes.

The man started talking without introducing himself or saying hello or good morning or thanks for coming or be quiet. He just started talking.

"Everything you need for today is inside the envelope. Take one and pass 'em around. Open 'em up and start readin'." He spoke in a deep voice tinged with a western twang. Everyone did as the man said and Lars thought about the new Hanson ski boots while he was waiting. Some of the guys at Dick's Ski Shop in Grayrock had said they were not very comfortable. Lars got the last envelope. Everybody was there. The man came to the back and nodded at Lars when he took the empty box back and he set it on the table at the front. He spoke again. It all seemed so professional to Lars.

"Read the short list of instructions. If you got any questions ask 'em right now. If your instructions are on a blue sheet of paper, you're on the blue course today. If it's red I think you can guess what course you're on."

Harry interrupted the sound of papers shuffling. "Hey! There's no lift ticket in here. Can we use the gate-keepers bib when we want to go skiing?"

"Y'all won't have time to go skiing today," came the response. "You'll get two complimentary passes when you turn your bib in at the end of the race in this room."

"But we want to ski today, man."

"Then you'll have to buy a ticket."

"That's twenty rotten bucks," Kent said to Carol. "I thought we'd ski for nothin'!" She kept looking straight ahead and all Lars could do was look at the curve of her neck running down to her shoulders with a ponytail of shiny hair splitting it on either side and he could tell she wasn't listening to Kent. The man spoke again, his voice a little sterner this time.

"Look, you punks, I couldn't give a shit what you think. Ya'll agreed to come out here. There's a free lunch in the cafeteria, just show 'em your bib. You'll get your passes later. If you don't wanna do this, just leave your envelope in the box on your way out."

The room went silent. Lars didn't mind not skiing today, even with all the new snow. He just wanted to watch the racers. And being a gatekeeper gave him the best seat in the house. He wondered which part of the course he would get and hoped it would be near one of the jumps. The man spoke again.

"You'll see a number on the top of that blue or red paper. The same number is on a big blue or red flag along the side of the course, starting with number one up near the start. You find your number on the course and you stand there. You look after all the gates on your side of the course between you and the next flag. No trading places and no goofing off."

Everybody started talking again, all wanting to find out where their friends and had ended up. Lars looked at the number on his paper and then leaned forward in his seat.

"Hey, I'm in B-7. Where are you, Kent?"

"What's it to you? Can't you see we're talking?"

Kent had not been talking and looked annoyed. Lars saw he had a red sheet of paper. Carol's was blue. She turned towards Lars, her ponytail swinging with the movement of her head.

"I'm in B-8," she said with a smile. "That's just below you. I'll need some help out there. What's your name?"

"You've picked the right one," Kent butted in. "Svensson's our official gatekeeper. He's just a manager."

"I wasn't talking to you," she said with an icy voice casting a glance towards Kent and then turned her pretty head back toward Lars with her hair swishing back and forth as if she enjoyed it. "I'm Carol."

"Lars. And I'm faster than he is in a course, already." Lars wished he hadn't said that as he was sure Kent would now try to slug him but the man spoke again to quiet everybody down.

"Read those race rules on the paper. If somebody misses a gate or falls in front of you, wave that flag and write his bib number down in the notebook. Just watch the racers' feet. They gotta get two feet past every pole," he said looking around the room nodding his head as though he was counting everybody there and then looked at his watch. "The first round starts in half an hour. Let's get moving," he concluded and walked over towards the door as if to usher everybody out, leaving the empty box on the table for anyone who dared not be a part of the Pro Race.

Everybody was standing up to put his or her coat back on and place the gatekeeper bib over the top. Kent and Carol were helping each other. Lars still sat in his seat, reading through the list of instructions. There were usual reminders just like the man had said. One rule that caught his attention was: "Do not speak to the racer, especially if they ski out of the course." This was completely different from high school because if someone fell or missed a gate they had to ask the gatekeeper where to go. Lars was impressed that high school rules and pro rules were so different. He sat there thinking that it must be a bit like the difference between high school and pro football, like when you were considered down if your knee touched the ground when carrying the ball in high school, even if nobody tackled you. In the pros it was definitely different.

He looked up and saw that everyone was out of the room now and the man was standing by the box waiting for him. Maybe the man was thinking he was considering not doing the gate keeping so Lars jumped up, stuffing the bib, notebook and small pencil into one pocket of his down-filled vest and folding the envelope up with the rules in it and tucking that into the other pocket. He walked past the man who nodded at him and Lars headed down the concrete stairs and into the cold air outside.

The light now had an intense brightness to it and the air seemed to be buzzing. It was going to be a great day for a race. Looking out towards the parking lots Lars saw streams of cars pouring in and hundreds of people walking towards the lodge, most of them carrying skis but some without any gear. He thought they must be spectators, wearing their fur coats and carrying umbrellas in case it snowed some more. He looked up the hill while walking with the other gate-keepers towards the McClouth chairlift station. The narrow, steep, tree-lined run called Hemlock stood directly above, fresh snow glistening in sunlight with a red course on the left and a blue course on the right looking up. Three huge jumps had been made by bulldozers to make one of the toughest runs in the state look even tougher.

Up in the trees along the left side of the course some people had climbed up and were trying to hang a huge banner. It was from the sweater manufacturer that always had advertisements in *Skiing* or *Ski* magazine where the models wore Band-Aid plasters on their faces. Lars could not figure out why they all had to wear Band-Aids and he hoped the guys hanging the banner in the leafless oak trees wouldn't fall, otherwise they might need Band-Aids. Looking further up this run called Hemlock Lars could sense the excitement of what was going to happen today and he was going to be a part of it. What he could not figure out was why a few years ago some vandals had cut down the huge Hemlock tree that stood at the top of the run. His thoughts were broken by the sound of a girl's voice behind him.

"You'd better put your bib on," the girl said quietly, tapping him on the shoulder and then stepping alongside him to add, "It'll look better that way."

"Sure," Lars replied and smiled at her as he reached in to the pocket of his down vest. "I thought you'd be up the hill already."

"I had to go to the bathroom and get my warm-ups," she replied and smiled sweetly at him. "We're going to be out here for a long time".

"Yeah, you're right," Lars said and thought to himself he probably should have gone himself. This girl not only looked good and skied good, she was also sensible. He began fumbling with the bib, trying to put it over his head and straighten it out as it was all twisted and inside-out now.

"Here, let me help you," she said and managed to straighten things out and began tying the cloth straps dangling at his side. He felt his heart beating faster with her standing so close to him, smelling so nice, looking so pretty. She was the same height as he was and he looked right into her pale blue eyes when she looked up after tying one side of the bib. He could hardly talk but he needed to say something.

"Thank you, Carol," was about all he could manage.

"No problem. So you ski for Grayrock? And you remembered my name."

"That's not hard. You're the best girl racer in this part of the state. And I don't ski for Grayrock, not yet. I'm just a manager."

Carol walked around Lars to tie the other strap and when she looked up again he could tell she was blushing a little, the tops of her clear-skin cheeks showing a touch of red.

"So what do you think about all this today?" she asked to make conversation.

"I think it's pretty exciting."

"Yeah, I can't wait to see the racing. I think we're in a good spot to watch from."

"We're probably just after the middle jump."

"How do you know that?"

"I was counting the number of flags alongside the course."

"And here I thought you were standing there daydreaming."

"I was doing a bit of that, too," Lars said, now his turn to blush. He felt like he was really dreaming now. He smiled at her and she smiled back, then spoke.

"Well, we'd better get up the hill and 'get to work,' as they say. Let's go. We'll ride up together."

Lars couldn't believe his luck. Here he was, walking beside this pretty girl from Gaylord toward the lift station. She was even talking to him as though he were the most important guy in the world. And here he was, at the top ski area in Michigan, about to be a part of the Pro Race. Some of the racers were coming down the run after having inspected the course. Others were heading over to the lift station, pairs of specially prepared race skis slung over shoulders. He didn't recognize any of them but at this time in the morning it was the qualifying round anyhow. He and Carol walked onto the boarding point together and the operator gave them a smile and said "Good morning, kids," before slowing the chair with his arm and then, "Have a good day up there," as he released it and they were heading up the hill together.

"This is a bit different," Carol said with a slight giggle, looking down and dangling her feet. "I've never been up a chairlift without skis on."

"Seems kinda strange, doesn't it?" Lars replied, looking at her and she smiled at him.

"Everything is just so exciting, but nothing like being in a race myself. I get so nervous."

"You get nervous before a race?"

"Oh yeah, real nervous sometimes. My legs feel like jelly, even if I'm in the lead after the first run."

Lars laughed to himself. His legs had felt like jelly standing beside her.

"What's so funny?"

"Nothing. I'm just surprised that you get nervous. You're so good."

"Not really. More like lucky. Anyhow, I'm not nervous now. I'm happy."

Lars could see that slight bit of color in her cheeks again and he smiled at her.

"I'm happy, too. Happy that I met you. Let's be friends." He had heard other girls say that to boys in the hallway at Grayrock high so he thought that would be something to try to say to her.

"That sounds like a good idea. You sound like a nice guy. You don't mind helping me with the gate-keeping?"

"Of course not. We'll have a lot of fun watching the race." Lars thought to himself he would like to have a lot of fun with this girl. She was looking over his shoulder at the course now so he turned his head away from looking at her and looked to see the racers inspecting the course. Some of them were peering over the precipice of the middle jump, looking down at a drop of over ten feet.

"Look at those jumps!" she said with excitement in her voice. "They are just so awesome."

"Yeah. I can't believe they're so big."

"Our coach said they used a bulldozer to make them last week."

"That's what I heard. Did you see it on the news last night?"

"I did! They had the interview with Jean-Claude Killy. Look, there he is now, up at the next jump!" She pointed up ahead of them.

Lars couldn't believe his eyes. There he was, standing at the crest of the jump, surveying the course. He looking tall, thin and relaxed in a blue outfit and blue hat, goggles resting on his forehead and the racing bib tight against his torso. The lift continued climbing upwards and they kept watching in silence until Lars spoke when they were level with the first jump.

"That's him, for sure."

"Doesn't he look cool?" Carol pleaded.

"I didn't think we'd see him out this early."

"Why not?"

"He doesn't have to qualify. He's one of the overall leaders. Everyone below the top sixteen has to qualify. The top times in the morning qualifying runs get to go head-to-head against the likes of Killy and Sabich. It's just straightforward elimination rounds right down to the final late this afternoon."

"Gosh Lars, you seem to know a lot about this."

"It's just what I read. I guess Killy's out there because he's such a professional."

"And he's just so handsome!" she said as they approached the lift station at the top. "C'mon, let's run down and see if we can meet him." They stood up to run off the lift and then slid down the hard snow on the off ramp and Carol lost her balance. He reached out to grab her just in time. She felt light and soft in his arms. She turned to smile at him.

"Thanks. I didn't want to end up on my rear end."

"Me neither. Try to slide a bit when you're going downhill, like you have short skis on or something."

They walked across the top of the run where it was flat. The place was filled with tents displaying ski company logos all in bright colors. Technicians were walking around frantically, carrying tools and rolls of cable. There was lots of shouting going on in all kinds of foreign accents. The pair of aluminum swinging doors that controlled the start was being tested. *Clang! Clang!* The doors shuddered on their 2 by 4 frames set into the snow. Lars could picture the racers hurtling out of the start, head to head towards the first gate of the parallel slalom.

He and Carol didn't hang around the chaotic start hut. They began walking down the steep slope alongside the course inside the red barrier erected to keep the spectators out.

There were other footprints in the snow and it was mashed up enough so that they could walk down without sliding. The course was right beside them and it looked steep and icy. Each turn was set with a pair of bamboo poles with a flag wired between them advertising the cigarette company. That was another difference to high school and for that matter even Olympic or World Cup racing. The racers just had to turn at the pole just like a practice course. It made things simple. They passed a man standing in a well and wearing headphones with one of the big TV cameras beside him. The camera bore the logo of the Network that showed *Wide World of Sports* every Sunday and during the winter televised some ski races, but they were taped and Lars knew the result from reading *Ski Racing* before it was telecast. But it would be good to watch this race again when it was shown because he was here, watching it live right now. The man was having difficulty and was swearing at whoever was listening to him: "Don't tell me your problems, dammit! The feed isn't working. Get your ass up here right away!"

Killy was standing in the course talking to another racer. Lars wasn't sure who it was but thought it was the Italian Renzo. They were speaking in French and Lars heard them say, "*Cette course est difficile.*" Killy was pointing towards the crest of the first jump. Lars and Carol walked past and Lars nodded at Killy but the nod was not returned. They kept walking downhill and when they got close enough to the jump Lars elbowed Carol and said, "Hey. Let's go check out the jump."

They both stood over the lip of the jump and looked down. It looked like a long way down, almost like they were standing on the roof of a house. Neither Carol nor Lars could say anything; they just stood there looking down from the jump to the next flag below them that the racers would have to probably turn in mid-air to make. Their silence was interrupted by shouts at them in some foreign language. They both turned around and saw Killy slide-slipping towards them, pushing his hands towards the snow as if trying to calm everything down.

"Eeets okay," he said. "Just be careful wis your boots." One of the other racers had been doing the shouting and he took off to ski past and around the jump and then rejoined the course, doing a few gates and then skiing out again.

"Is he allowed to do that?" Carol asked. Lars looked at Carol and knew what she was thinking. If you even attempted to practice skiing through any gates in a high school course you would get disqualified.

"Eeets okay," Killy said again, adding, "Eet won't matter."

Another racer skied down, making relaxed casual turns before coming to a stop at the lip of the jump. It was Spider Sabich. He was wearing an old down jacket with bits of duct tape mending rips and he wore a white wool hat with a pig and a pair of skis on it. He was smiling and spoke to Killy. Lars thought he was on a movie set.

"Hey JC, how's it goin'?"

"Eeets okay."

"Is that all you can say? I heard you had a pretty wild night."

Killy laughed. "*Oui. Ces femmes du Michigan, ce sont de vrai folles!*"

Spider Sabich laughed with him. "You can say that again." Lars was listening to them and he wondered what they were talking about. Then they got back to business.

"Wadda think of the course?"

"Eeets tough. Theese first jump is a beetch."

"Naw, just another day at the office. Think I'll kick your ass today."

"Ve'll zee."

A deep voice came over the loudspeakers placed up and down the Hemlock run: "All gatekeepers in position right now! Racers clear the course! Heats start in five minutes!"

"Guess we'd better get a move on," Lars said to Carol. She nodded back at him but then shifted her gaze back to the two racers.

"Hey you kids!" Spider Sabich shouted at them. "Thanks a lot for coming out today! Have fun and don't disqualify me!"

Killy smiled at Carol and nodded at Lars and said, "*Oui, merci.*"
Lars and Carol both waved back and said "good luck" in unison and
began walking down the hill again.

They were nearly at the spot where Lars was to position himself to
watch the course, just below the middle jump. Neither had said a
word until Lars pointed to his blue flag along the side of the course
and he told Carol, "Here's where I get off. If you need any help just
shout."

"Isn't he a dreamboat?" Carol replied, her blue eyes now looking a
bit misty.

"What's that?"

"Spider. He's just so handsome. Now I see how he got that
crooner's wife."

"What's a crooner?"

"Oh, you know, he's the one who does those Christmas songs."

"Oh yeah," Lars said smiling, amazed that this girl was putting up
with his stupidity. "Well Carol, I'll come down to talk to you in a
while if we're not too busy."

"Sure Lars," she said sweetly. "That would be fine."

He watched her walk down the slope while he tried to figure out
what she was talking about.

The heats started with the racers going head-to-head against each
other. They were also racing against the clock to get the sixteen fastest times. Several of them fell at the first jump, catching too much air
coming off the lip of the jump and either crashing into the gate
below it or missing it entirely. It was just like Killy had said. The ones
that did make it came streaking past him carrying good speed after
the second jump. The better ones would drive their knees and shoulders into the bamboo poles and Lars could hear the loud crack of
bamboo snapping in both courses. He was so close to the course that
he could see the expressions of determination on their faces. They

didn't even seem to flinch from the pain that must have come from striking the bamboo with their body. Whenever Lars hit a gate in practice his shoulders, knees or thighs hurt for days. These guys probably didn't even notice.

The course was taking a beating. All of the gatekeepers were out to reset the flags after each run. One of the Boyne Mountain ski instructors had stopped to help Carol. Lars was too busy to make it down to help her but she would smile up at him when they had the course repaired for the next set of racers. He used one of his old tricks of swapping the two gates around so that a fresh piece of bamboo was there for the turning gate. After several runs the bamboo wrapped in colored electrical tape was in splinters. Occasionally someone would come over the public address to give out the times and they said that a young racer named Perry Thompson with the skis that had the hexagons on them had the fastest time in the qualifying round. They were told there would be a break in the action and a chance for the gatekeepers to repair the course before the next round started. Lars grabbed some of the spare poles set in the snow alongside the course and went to work.

Music was playing loudly over the PA as Lars worked on the course. The snow was holding up well, nice and firm but not icy. He looked down at Carol who was attempting to do the same tasks as Lars and further up the hill to Kent and Harry over on the red course. People were now making their way up the hill, coming out of the lodge and gathering in the finish area. Groups of skiers were stopping alongside the course and taking their skis off, having decided on a place to watch from. Lars could hear the sound of a microphone crackling and then a deep familiar voice boomed out:

"Ladies and Gentlemen! This is Bob Beattie at race time! You know I love the weather forecasts here in the Midwest. Don't you just enjoy waking up to a foot of 'partly cloudy'!"

A few people standing alongside the course laughed at that. Lars looked over and saw a group of women, all about the same age as his math teacher Miss Jenkins. Miss Jenkins wasn't married yet and Lars would see her riding around Grayrock occasionally, sitting as close as possible to different men in different cars on different days. She also talked and joked with some of the bigger seniors on the football team, laughing just like that group of women were doing. Lars looked down the hill to see numerous cameras being set up, all with long lenses. One of them was aiming his camera at Carol who was struggling with a gate, trying to pull it out of the snow. Lars had finished his repairs and started heading down to help Carol. He heard the commentator coming over the PA again.

"We've got some great racing for you today, folks. Just as soon as the parade of flags comes down this challenging course we'll start the round of thirty-two racers going head-to-head in this challenging slalom here at, uh, Boyne Mountain. The fastest time from our qualifying round earlier this morning is paired against the slowest time. They'll each do a run in the red course on the right and then the blue course on the left. Whoever has the best overall time advantage goes to the next round. If a racer falls or skis out in the first run he's given a 1.5-second handicap to try and make up in the second." Lars had made it down to Carol by now and began helping her. One of the splintered bamboo poles was stuck deep into the snow and Lars had to pull with all his might to get it out. He managed and then Carol slid a new pole into the hole.

"Isn't this exciting, Lars?" she asked.

"I've got goose bumps all over me," Lars replied and they smiled at each other. "Why don't you tie that flag on," he said and reached into the pocket of his down vest. "Here's some spare wires. I'll go down to the next gate. It needs changing, too."

"Thanks, Lars—I knew I could rely on you," Carol said and they just stood there smiling at each other, standing on this course at the Pro Race. The commentator boomed his voice out again.

"The sixteen winners from this round will go up against the top pro racers in the world! We have some great newcomers on the tour this year. You hot-blooded Italian women out there will want to keep your eye out for a real live hot-blooded Italian racer, Renzo." Lars heard cheering from the crowd and he looked back up the hill and saw that group of likely single schoolteachers probably up from Bay City were laughing and cheering and passing around a wineskin. The commentator continued:

"Speaking about hot, we've got some of the best racers in the world battling it out for the overall title today. You all know that Jean-Claude Killy is here today." The crowd responded with a roar. The commentator paused and continued: "But leading the championship so far is our own Spider Sabich. Aside from being a great racer and fun person, Spider seems to be a bit like a magnet. Why, he was just telling me about it the other night! While standing around in a crowded finish area after the race in Stowe last week, he reached into the pocket of that old down jacket he's wearing today. Inside he found six hotel room keys, all planted by some of his admirers!"

The crowd roared with laughter and then the commentator said the parade of flags was about to begin along with the playing of the National Anthem. Lars had never heard the Star Spangled Banner being played before a ski race. The national flag of each country represented by a racer was paraded and the crowd went quiet except for the schoolteachers who were still laughing and giggling about the hotel key incident.

"What a great idea!" He heard one of them say loudly.

"I wouldn't mind putting something in his pocket," giggled another, just as loud.

"Yeah, but not in his jacket," Came another silly comment. Lars felt an elbow nudge him. He turned to see Carol had walked down and was standing beside him.

"We'd better hurry up, they'll be starting the next round," she said.

"You're right, Carol. We can just stay here while those flag carriers ski past us," he said and looked up to see one of the Boyne ski instructors carrying an Austrian flag. He was followed by others skiing down making big sweeping slow turns in and around the course carrying flags of all the different countries. Lars went back to work and helped Carol rewire the flags back onto the poles. She was standing next to him and kept looking at him and smiling.

"Thanks for helping me, Lars. You're pretty good at this."

"No problem."

She looked down at the snow as if thinking about what to say next and then came out with it.

"What are you going to do with your free tickets?"

"Don't know yet. Probably come up sometime in March if the snow holds out. Depends on who I can get to take me."

"I've got an idea. My older brother, he goes out with Marci Kelly from Grayrock. You know her?" Lars nodded. Marci was a junior ski patroller out at the hill.

"When's he's back from Tech they always go skiing. It might cost you one of your free passes, but it would be worth it!"

"You don't think they'd mind?"

"Of course not. I'll call you. I'll get your phone number later."

Lars gulped. "Does this mean it's a date?"

"Let's just call it friends going skiing," she said giving him a wink of one of her beautiful eyes.

The last of the skiers went past carrying the Star and Stripes. Lars felt tingling all over his body and he stood at attention next to Carol and took his hat off and listened to the National Anthem and just could not believe how lucky he was. He went back to his position and watched the round of thirty-two go by in a blur, spending more time looking down at Carol. When the round had finished they were told there would be a one-hour break for lunch. He had already written his phone number down on a piece of paper from the small notebook for disqualifying racers. He tore the page out and gave it to Carol and asked if he could join her for lunch. She smiled and said of course and they walked down the hill together and went inside the crowded cafeteria. All of the gatekeepers got to sit together at a big table reserved for them and they were all talking to each other about the race so far. Lars didn't mind Kent talking to Carol about Spider Sabich and his French girlfriend and the singer. He quietly ate his cheeseburger and French fries and gave Carol an occasional glance and he could tell she was looking at him when he was looking somewhere else.

When they came out after lunch the sky was still bright and the lift lines were huge.

The lift operator shouted and waved for the gatekeepers to come through the ski instructors' chute, which gave them a shortcut to the loading point. The operator would hold up the paying customers every so often and let a pair of gatekeepers board and he'd repeat himself saying, "These kids gotta get back up for the race." There were occasional groans from the crowd waiting to go up the hill and Lars overheard a few comments like, "They should of stayed out on the hill." Lars didn't mind; in fact, he felt pretty good about using the instructor's lane and even better that he could go up with Carol and talk to her. But his hopes were shattered when the operator shouted for Carol to come forward and pair up with a single, saying, "C'mon, he ain't gonna bite you." Carol boarded, looking back at Lars who by now was the last gatekeeper to go.

"You wait for the next single," the operator said but Lars barely heard him. He just stood there looking up the hill watching Carol ride away from him. He felt like he'd never see her again and lost his chance and there were so many things he wanted to say to her and then he heard a voice behind him that he faintly recognized.

"Hey kid, you just gonna stand there?"

Lars turned around to see Spider Sabich standing behind him, wearing that same down jacket, that hat with the pig insignia, that same disarming smile on a face that needed a shave. He was sliding his skis back and forth as though he were a little impatient.

"Let's let this racer and gatekeeper up the lift, folks," the operator said, holding up the moving queue and motioning to the pair of them to board.

"Yeah, I'm ready—let's go," Lars said and walked out to the boarding point and Spider Sabich was soon sitting beside him heading towards the top of Boyne Mountain for the Pro Race; but all Lars could do was look ahead to where Carol was sitting, about five chairs between them. He watched her turning around to look back, that ponytail of shiny hair swishing and a smile on her face gleaming. Lars gave her a wave and then looked down at the skis Spider Sabich would be racing on. They were K2 models that he hadn't seen before. The surface had the parallel red white and blue stripes but also white pin stripes running through the darker colors.

"You like those K2s?" Lars asked, wanting to start the conversation.

"Yeah. You ought to try them. Any good American racer should be on K2s," came the response in a friendly tone but Lars felt embarrassed by asking. He was skiing on Rossignol Stratos. Killy raced on Rossingnols.

"Our local shop doesn't have K2s. I've never seen those ones before."

"Hell, you can get these almost anywhere. They'll be out next year. You'll like 'em."

"I'll try to look for them."

"Do you race?"

"Yeah. Well no—not yet. I practice with the high school team. I'll race next year. I'm only in eighth grade."

"I raced in high school. It was great. Got to meet lots of girls. Tell me, do you go to school with her or did you just meet today?"

"I've seen her around at races. She goes to another school. She's a pretty good racer."

"I kinda figured that. She's pretty cute. Do ya like her?"

"Yeah, I do. So far. But I don't know what to do. I mean like, I want to be a racer. But I also want to be with girls."

"Listen kid, I know how you feel. They only want to mess you around, tie you around their little finger. Here's what you do. You practice hard, you leave those bitches alone for a while. If you get good at it, then you can tell them what to do. Until then, you're playing right into their hands."

Lars thought for a moment. He was actually getting advice from one of the top pro racers in the world. Advice he would never get at home or from his friends.

"Is that what you did, to make it to the pros, Mr Sabich?"

"C'mon. Call me Spider. Only bellboys call me Mr Sabich." He slooked Lars right in the eye and continued. "Yeah, we all have to make sacrifices but believe me, it'll pay off one day."

"But what about that business with the hotel keys? The stuff Mr Beattie was talking about?"

"Uncle Bob? He says that every weekend. But hey, that's exactly what I mean. If you work hard, they'll be coming to you one day. But don't expect that to happen on its own."

"What about that French woman, you know, the one whose old man does the songs?"

"You read too many gossip columns, kid. She's around, just like the rest of 'em. Worry about that if you get there. You've gotta earn it."

"I'll try real hard."

"You have to do more than that. You have to make it your life. No hangin' out at the beach in the summer. Take it easy on the partying and the women."

"I don't drink. And I don't have a girlfriend. Not yet anyhow."

"Want some advice? Keep it that way. And keep believing in yourself. It'll all fall into place."

The lift was now approaching the summit and Sabich got ready to get off the lift. Lars jumped off at the same time, shouting, "Good luck and thanks for the advice!"—but he wasn't sure if Sabich heard him. Kent and Carol watched him ski past and waited for Lars to walk over to where they stood at the top of the course. Carol spoke first, sounding pretty excited.

"What did he *say* to you?! Did you get his autograph?"

"Naw, we just talked about racing."

"That must not have taken long, based on what you know," Kent said in his most caustic tone.

Lars didn't reply. He just started walking down the hill towards his place along the course, thinking all the while that he did know something now.

A few years later Lars saw Spider's picture on the cover of *Ski Racing*. He had come home from a good afternoon of training over at Mont Ripley. He knew that Spider was dead as it made the news on the Marquette station a few nights ago. He still couldn't believe it and didn't expect to see his picture on the cover. He was wrong about that but felt right about his own life as he looked at the black and white photo of a face that hadn't changed since that afternoon on a chairlift at Boyne Mountain. It was quiet in the small house on Houghton Avenue that he shared with his cousins, all of them now studying engineering at Michigan Tech. He slung his backpack heavy with books over his shoulder and walked up to his bedroom, carrying the magazine and the rest of his unopened mail. He looked out the window at the snow covered hills across the Portage and over to Ripley now in twilight.

He stood there thinking while looking at the cover of a magazine sitting on the desk. Below the picture was Spider's name and the years of his time on earth. Just like on a tombstone. He thought back to that exciting afternoon at Boyne Mountain, Killy just beating Spider in the final of the slalom.

Lars and Carol never did make that skiing date. He'd have to remind her of all that at the race this coming weekend. She skied for Northern Michigan now and she had a good chance to qualify for the National Collegiate finals. He felt he had a pretty good chance too and wanted to get to the NCAAs in Steamboat. He'd had lots of chances with Carol and lots of other girls but had no regrets about not going further with any of them. He didn't bother to open the magazine to see if they'd published his article on the Midwest collegiate skiing circuit. He had too many other things on his mind.

The Professor

The sound of knocking at the hotel room door startled me, even though I was ready. I was in the bathroom at the other end of the room, putting some zinc oxide on my lips. Running across the big room towards the door in the dark I nearly stumbled on somebody's clothes strewn on the floor. Bright morning light bathed the darkened room when I pulled the door open and the big burly shape of the Coach in his green down jacket and raccoon-like eyes stepped over the threshold. My roommates all tossed about in their beds and tried to go back to sleep. Coach Wisner reached down to grab my ski boots and I grabbed my backpack crammed full of all my stuff.

"Looks like you've got everything as usual, Svensson," the Coach said softly, which surprised me because he was usually shouting at us.

"I was going to leave it in the truck, coach. My lunch is in there." I kept my voice down but saw my teammate Jim sit up in bed. "Always prepared, just like a Boy Scout."

"You wanna close that door?" Jim said towards us, rubbing his eyes.

"Certainly, Mr Head—wouldn't want to interrupt your beauty sleep," the Coach said sarcastically towards him, then turned to me: "C'mon Lars, let's get going. Everyone else is waiting in the truck. You got goggles or sunglasses in there?"

"Yessir," I replied, hoisting the backpack over my shoulder and looking back at Jim as I closed the door. The other two roommates were sleeping soundly in their beds. I nodded at Jim and said, "See you later."

"Have a good run," he replied and crawled back under the covers.

The big Suburban truck was idling away in the parking lot just in front of our rooms at this hotel high in Summit County. All of the other cars and vans we had come out in sat parked in the row opposite the rooms, quiet and empty, windows frosted. In a few hours everybody else would be waking up and piling out of their rooms and loading up to head up the pass for a final day's worth of skiing at Arapahoe Basin. By the time they got to the parking lot at 10,000 feet we'd be skiing down through the powder on the mountain opposite. That mountain was called The Professor. We were going to drive to the top of Loveland Pass early on this fine April morning, walk up for over an hour and then ski down through the powder with everybody watching from the parking lot. It was going to be a great Good Friday.

But we had to get up there first. I opened the back door of the Suburban and tossed my bag in, then climbed in on top of all the other bags. The rest of the seats had been taken by the others crazy enough to get up at six to drive, hike, and make a single run down a Colorado mountain. Counting the Coach, there were seven of us going for the run, but only two others were my teammates off the Grayrock high school team. They were both seniors and were already chatting to Carol who lived in Gaylord and was already perched in the front seat. All of our skis were set in the roof rack and I had the company of seven pairs of poles, a few small bags, loose ski boots, and a coil of rope.

Mr. Brock was already sitting behind the steering wheel of the Coach's truck. He must have volunteered to take us up the pass and then come back down to Dillon and then wait for everybody else back at the hotel, only to drive back up the pass to A-Basin all over again.

His son Carl sat in front of me in the middle seat. Carl wasn't much of a skier but was a good football player, All-State Honorable Mention as a defensive safety. He was going to West Point and Coach had convinced him to come out to Colorado on this skiing trip. Coach had always said that you could only play football for so long but you could ski for the rest of your life. Up in the front seat Coach and Mr Brock were talking about the NFL draft. I already knew there were no players from West Point selected. Carl turned around to talk to me as the Suburban backed out of the parking lot.

"Did you watch the game last night?" he asked.

"Yeah—that's Babe Ruth's record gone now," I replied, picturing the scene of Hank Aaron slamming his 716th Home Run over the left field fence in some empty ballpark.

"I wonder if he'll retire."

"I don't think anyone cares," I observed. "Didn't look like there were many people at the game." I had managed to catch the Braves playing on the NBC Game of the Week after skiing before going to the PJ's Pizza for dinner. None of the guys in my room were particularly interested either. They didn't play baseball.

"No, I kinda thought the same. Seemed like it would be more special than it was."

"You gonna play Legion Ball this summer?" I asked, thinking about Carl's hanging curveball.

"Yeah, if I can fit it in. After the high school season I'll try to get a few games in. I suppose you'll be trying out for tennis again this year instead."

"And working. In the storeroom at The Mart. I start nights and weekends when we get back."

"Well, at least you'll have your pick of good looking girls. Old man Krosier is quite a ladies man."

"I found out they all come from Rosco. Guess they're all related. What you gonna do?"

"I'll probably work at the lumberyard when I can and play ball up until July," Carl announced. "Then I have to report." He looked out at the mountain scenery. We were out on the road now and climbing up the pass approaching the turnoff into Keystone.

"Oh," I replied, and realized their conversation was over. That was probably the most Carl had ever spoken to me. I sat there in the back end of the truck and wondered if Carl was being talkative because he was excited about going up The Professor or was excited about going to West Point or was just plain nervous about all of it.

As the truck rolled along, laboring now as it felt the long uphill grade, I thought about those girls I'd seen in The Mart before. I always wondered where they came from, with their summer suntans and looking good in tight fitting white polyester trousers and thin see-through yellow shirts. I never realized that they came from Roscommon, but that didn't matter to me. The girl I was interested in was back at our hotel in Dillon, probably still asleep with her roommates, all of them on the girls' team but none of them very good racers. That didn't matter either as Judy was good looking and I was hoping she would be looking at me as I came down that Professor later this morning. I tried to picture her in the parking lot, wearing those tight new green ski pants and the sun glistening off her face and maybe smiling and maybe spending some time with me skiing today after we finished our run down The Professor.

The truck was rolling past the parking lot now with the sign for 10,000 feet behind us and the hairpin bends and steeper climb ahead of us. I was still wondering about those girls in their white and yellow see-through uniforms and why they came from Roscommon and if I would have to wear white as well at The Mart when the Coach's deep voice caught my attention. Everyone was looking back at me and I knew they wanted an answer to a question I hadn't heard.

"I said Svensson, did you bring a camera or not? Are you deaf?"

"C'mon coach, cantcha tell he's in love? He's been daydreaming about Judy Binns all week!" Larry Klinsman remarked, generating laughs from everyone else in the truck.

The girl from Gaylord turned and cast a smile and managed to give me a wink when nobody was looking. Carol Winters looked good in the morning light, her blonde hair in a ponytail. From where I sat her eyes reflected off the big rear view mirror mounted on the windshield. I could look at that reflection all day but I had to answer the coach.

"Yessir, I've got one. It's in my backpack."

"Good, Svensson. You can leave everything else behind. Just take that camera. I want you to get some good shots."

"Hey Svensson, you gonna do anything on this trip for the school paper?" Scott Shield asked.

Scott was another football player, another senior who didn't want to go to college but wanted to move out West after graduation. It was his first time in the Rockies and he had told everybody he couldn't wait to graduate and move out here. Lars gave him a friendly shrug of his shoulders. He hadn't thought about doing any writing but it was a good idea. Scott always had good practical ideas and was a natural leader out on the football field, playing middle linebacker. He was also pretty good with a chainsaw, having worked in his Dad's logging company each summer. He made enough money cutting down trees to buy a good used pickup and new skiing equipment. Being a big affable and capable guy, he'd probably have no problem finding a job as a logger out here—and there were a lot of big trees on these mountainsides on the way up Loveland Pass, and just about everywhere else in Central Colorado.

"Well?" Carl asked for an answer to this question.

"I dunno," I replied. "The thing is, skiing season is over with. Nobody will want to read about skiing with the grass growing and everyone playing baseball or tennis."

"You're probably right, Lars," Carl said. "By the time you get another issue of that paper out we'd have forgotten about this trip."

A few other passengers laughed. Carl was right. The Grayrock student paper *Runes* came out on an irregular basis, many times depending on how many articles I had written and how much advertising I had sold. Funny thing was, I'd met Krosier at the Mart trying to sell advertising space and that's how I got offered the job there.

"Hey, there's been nothing wrong with this trip!" exclaimed Carol, turning around again and looking at all the boys crammed together in the middle. "I've had a great time," she announced and cast another glance above their heads towards me in the back. We had skied together yesterday afternoon up above the tree line. I spent much of the time trying to get her confidence up to make this run down the Professor. I had also told her about my affections for Judy and asked her for advice, as Judy was playing hard to get and Carol seemed so friendly and mature to me now.

"I wasn't meaning the trip, Carol," Carl said. "I was talking about Svensson's paper. We hardly see a copy of it."

"Well, that's better than Gaylord. We don't even have one. They're talking about one for next year but I'll be long gone." She turned back towards the front. Mountain scenery passed by in all its bigness but all I could do was look at those eyes reflecting off the rear view mirror. They were just so clear and bright and beautiful.

"You still going to go to Northern?" Tom Norton asked to break the silence. Tom was a senior too, getting a chance to race in his last year. He fell in nearly every race. Carol turned around towards his acne-filled face to answer. Her ponytail swished about and touched the Coach's head sitting next to her and he brushed it aside.

"Yes, Tom, I am. And I presume you'll be there next year, too?"

"I still haven't decided yet, Carol. Are you still going to ski?"

The coach interrupted. "Of course she is. Northern's coach phoned both me and her coach to ask our opinion. Carol's been offered an athletic scholarship, haven't you Carol?"

Carol replied quietly, "Well, yes, I have. But it's only a small one, only for one year and renewed only if I make the team."

"I don't think there's any doubt about that," the coach replied deadpan and looked ahead. They were nearing the top of the pass. Carol turned back towards me again. Her face was a bit red even though she was developing a tan from a week up in the mountain sun.

"I was thinking about studying Journalism, Lars. You didn't tell me you were a writer." I could tell everybody else was listening intently.

"I'm not," I replied, wanting to tell her the truth. We had spoken the truth to each other yesterday skiing and I didn't want to change that.

"Maybe we could talk about it on the way back. I'd like to know what it's like to be a writer and have to do newspapers."

"Sure, why not?" I said with a smile. "Maybe we'll work on an article about this skiing trip after all."

"Sounds like you got yourself a date, Svensson," Carl said in a cocky voice and everybody burst out laughing at the thought of it, picturing me and Carol Winters, the best looking girl by far on this trip (next to Judy of course) and certainly the best girl at skiing. That's why she was asked if she wanted to do the Professor. I thought better of it, as I would rather have been sitting next to Judy on the way home and tried to talk her into going out with me. But it was a long trip and we'd be swapping cars around at each stop for gas so maybe I'd still have my chance with Judy.

"Looks like you've talked yourself into that one, Svensson," the coach said loudly over the laughing. Carol continued to look at me with a big smile on her face and I was going to say something to these guys like 'very funny' or 'that's no way to treat a lady'—but I didn't as the Suburban pulled off the road and into the parking lot at the top of Loveland Pass and the coach announced an end to the proceedings by announcing: "We're here. Let's get our gear on and get going."

Larry stepped around to open the back door and let me out. He just nodded at me and shook his head. The only words he spoke were, "Lars, you really are something else." I said thanks for opening the door and stood out on the hard packed snow of the parking area. Mr Brock had turned the ignition off and all was quiet for a few moments. I looked out at the spectacular mountain scenery. We were up at over 13,000 feet and still had more to climb to get to the top of the Professor. But it already felt like we were on the top of the world looking out at white snow and black rock in the sunshine. The Coach and Carl started taking skis off the roof rack and laying them on the snow. I started passing out bags and ski boots to everybody and we began to get ready. It didn't take long before everybody was standing around with ski boots on, some with small backpacks, all with skis and poles at their sides and ready to go. The roof racks were closed and we all said thanks to Mr Brock for driving us up the pass. I decided to take a few pictures while the coach was putting the coil of climbing rope over his shoulder. He spoke to all of us as if we were getting ready for a big ballgame.

"In case you're wondering what this rope is for, it's just a precaution. We spotted a crevasse forming up on the summit last year. Don't know what to expect this year. I spoke to some patrollers over at the lodge yesterday and they said conditions are good, little risk of avalanche or the like. Let's move out."

The coach took the lead and headed off towards the high snow bank at the edge of the parking area. Carl followed right behind him. I turned around and watched Mr Brock step back into the truck, fire up the engine and drive off. I gave him a wave but he didn't notice, the truck just headed off back down the pass.

The steady drone of an engine laboring interrupted the quiet mountain morning. I stood there looking while the others were queuing up in a line to march through the gap in the snow bank.

Carol stood next to me and we watched as a big semi truck came into view, creeping slowly towards the summit of the pass. The trailer it was towing had orange and black signs marked "Danger—Explosives" hanging from its sides. I was startled when the truck driver blew his horn, a deep reverberating blast that echoed around the mountain summits. Carol and I gave him a wave and the bearded driver blew a kiss, shifting gears and letting the truck roll on down the pass.

"I'll bet he's glad to have made the summit with that load," Carol remarked.

"He'll feel even better when he gets down the other side," I replied.

"I take it that they wouldn't let him through the tunnel carrying explosives"

"Just a precaution, as Coach would say. Besides, there's a big molybdenum mine down past Leadville."

"Speaking of your Coach, he'll be wondering what we're doing. We'd better get a move on."

"I kinda figured I'd be taking up the rear anyhow, Carol," I said and added, "After you." I said motioned with a ski pole towards the gap in the snow bank, slinging my Kniessel Red Stars over my shoulder. Carol did the same with her Volkl Sapporos and she said something like, "You're such a gentleman," as I watched her set off in those tight fitting shiny yellow and blue ski pants that the Gaylord girls wore. I was glad I was following her as it gave me something nice to look at besides the spectacular mountain scenery. I put my sunglasses on and felt good on this Good Friday as we began our ascent.

It didn't take long to catch up to the others. They were marching single file behind the Coach with that rope slung over his shoulder. He looked a bit like one of those Mexican characters in a spaghetti Western movie. Coach was pretty good to be taking us up this mountain, a real treat for all of those seniors. I was glad to be tagging along and tried to stay out of their way. In fact, I was pretty grateful to coach for organizing the whole trip. It had done my skiing a lot of good and improved my friendships. I only wished that I could be a better friend with Judy. No use thinking about her now. I just marched on over the hard-packed snow that ran up a ridge towards the summit of the Professor.

The trail was pretty well marked by piles of flat slabby stones. When it snowed it was probably well used by the ski bums coming up from Denver. We had seen them when we drove in last Saturday afternoon, coming through the Eisenhower Tunnel and entering a world of white and towering mountains. The ski bums were all out hitchhiking lifts back up from Loveland to the other side of the pass for a run down and they were probably doing the same thing here on the Professor. That was the last day it had snowed and we had not seen anybody ski down all week. I climbed on with plenty of energy knowing that our tracks would be the first and probably last ones of the day. It really didn't matter to me what the snow conditions were like—this was the chance of a young lifetime to enjoy.

We all kept hiking upwards on the hard crusty snow. The path made by everyone ahead of me was chiseled out into tiny narrow steps from their ski boots. Traction was good in the hard snow and I didn't slip or stumble. Occasionally I would have to stop as someone in the line would pause to reposition skis over shoulders or try to catch a quick breath, pretending to stop to look at the scenery. I would do the same; mainly to enjoy the views of what for me seemed like the top of the world.

But after a while the thin mountain air began to take its toll. We had probably been going for over a half hour when the march stopped. The coach walked back down a few feet to be midway along the line-up of us and he began his address after setting his Head Standards down on to the snow, resting them against his shoulder. We all did the same and I could see some of the gang breathing heavily. I lifted my sunglasses up onto the top of my head.

"If we look from here you can see just about everything in Summit County. You all know that A-Basin is just down there in front of us. Some of you ought to recognize the runs you've been doing all week. If you look immediately down the pass you can see Keystone. Further in the distance is Breckenridge. And the one back in line behind Keystone is Copper."

"Where's Vail?" Scott asked. He wanted to know where all the landmarks of Central Colorado where.

"Won't be able to see that till we reach the summit, so let's move out," he said, putting those skis he only used on 'powder days' over his shoulder.

"Oh, one more thing," he announced as he moved back to the front of the line, the coil of rope dangling over his shoulder. "Turn around and look straight out to where you can see where they've cut the trees down to resemble a cross. That's where that plane with the football team crashed a few years ago."

We all turned to look and I spotted it and pointed with a ski pole in the direction of the landmark and Carol leaned against my shoulder as if to be guided by my pointing. I felt her body against mine and it was warm and pulsating from her heavy breathing. She was beginning to look tanned and healthy and just so…, well so alive early on this Good Friday morning. She had perched her sunglasses up on her forehead.

"What a tragedy," she said and looked at me.

"I know. But having a bad crash out skiing doesn't make you stop," I replied and looked into her eyes. It suddenly occurred to me that I ought to be doing the same thing to Judy. I wished she were here with me now. But Judy wasn't here and I was on this mountain with this beautiful healthy young woman and I felt so high and mixed up I didn't know what to think or say anymore. Carol spoke.

"You are a handsome young man, Lars. You and Judy would make a cute couple."

"I hope so. Thanks for saying that, Carol. I just hope it happens. Do you want it to happen to you?"

"Oh, all girls are waiting for it to happen to them, and when it happens they least expect it. But I suppose something will happen when I'm up at Northern, at some party or ski race."

"What about right now?" I asked out of nowhere.

"What, you and me?" she gave a nervous little laugh and looked up the slope where the others were already tramping upwards and then returned the gaze. "We'll maybe talk about that later. Right now we'd better be catching up." She put her sunglasses back on and slung her skis over her shoulder and began climbing. I stood there looking at her, not believing I'd said that. I shook my head and did the same.

The final ascent was steep and we were all breathing heavily and making short steps in the hard snow. It had started to warm up and by the time the next half hour was gone I must have had a good sweat running. But it was still early and not near as hot as it had been out on the mountain all week. I thought I would be more tired and winded from the altitude. Maybe all those iron tablets and distance running back in Michigan had helped after all. Our pace slowed and I could see we were approaching the summit, marked by a large pile of flat brown stones. The group seemed to spread out from the single file line into a scattered one, all taking different directions across the hard icy snowfield towards the summit. I walked alongside Carol and tried to encourage her along. She was panting but trying to conceal it.

"Deep breaths, Carol. Get some oxygen in those lungs." I looked at her chest and breasts heaving up and down.

"Take my skis, would you? I... I can't go on any longer."

"Sure," I said. "Almost there Carol. Let me help you." I took the skis from her and patted her backside softly as though to encourage her and she looked at me and gave a weak smile between the heavy gasps. I saw a few beads of perspiration on her forehead and she indignantly stepped onwards leaving me holding the skis. I saw the others now all standing up at the summit setting their skis down and then lying down on the hard snow at the summit. I followed along and joined them, lying down next to Carol who was still breathing heavily, sucking in air as I suggested. I watched her chest rise and fall quickly and severely at first and then calmer and softer as she recovered. Then I closed my eyes and lay there listening to the sound of my heart pumping.

Then there was no sound. We all just lay there quietly, nobody speaking. Just that clear cool silence that can only exist on the top of a mountain. With my eyes still closed I tried to picture those mountains all around us, and mountains in other parts of the world and wondered if they were as beautiful. Maybe I'd find out one day. I opened my eyes and looked out at the mountains and then at Carol's body, calmer now but her chest still rising and falling. All God's creations, all there for me and others to enjoy. I felt determined now that I would make the best of it.

Then I thought about what day it was. Somewhere far away to the East, away from these snow-covered, sun-drenched mountains people would be gathering—believers thinking and praying about all the bad things in the world and how they were saved from their sins because they believed. With all this creation around me I knew I could believe now, too. I said a quiet little prayer and gave my own thanks. Then I enjoyed the silence for what seemed a very long time and I was happy.

I heard coach getting up first quietly and speaking softly, then louder as my colleagues started moving around to get ready. The silence had ended and it was time to ski.

"We have to head down this ridge and then across the saddle there. You'll need to keep your speed up otherwise it's a long push to the other side. It'll still be pretty hard snow until we get over there. The powder will be waiting on the north slope, for sure."

"And so will everybody else—waiting that is, down in the parking lot," Carl said. looking at his watch. I almost expected to hear him say, "move out" or whatever military types say in these circumstances.

"Hey look!" Scott exclaimed while wandering around the pile of rocks at this summit. "There's a whole pile of driver's licenses here!" he bent down and uncovered a rock and held up a stack of small laminated cards.

"That's a real tradition of the Professor," Coach explained, putting his skis on. He continued: "People leave their driver's licenses or business cards here. Maybe they hope they'll meet somebody here. I think the gays use it a lot."

"Gay or not, there's a few Colorado addresses here. Think I'll make a swap. I've still got my temporary license in my wallet." Scott fished out his wallet from his ski pants. We watched him swapping the cards around and I wondered just what sort of people he'd meet through that method. Probably ones just as crazy as us!

The coach slid over towards me and stood over me, holding onto the coil of rope. I stood up, having finished securing my powder straps. He lifted the coil of rope ceremoniously over my head and rested it on my shoulders as though it were a medal. Then he spoke quietly.

"You'll go last, Svensson. Ski steady. If there is any trouble you'll have to deal with it."

My thoughts were going from that of being honored to carry the rope for the Coach to ones of dreading the chore of skiing all the way down the Professor with this rope around my shoulder. But the Coach relieved me by saying not to worry and that he'd take the rope back from me when we got to the top of the run. Then he invited me and the others to look at the route to the run.

We looked down the long slope towards the saddle. A large cornice was hunched over the north edge and then a steep slope ran down below it. The saddle was only about twenty feet wide at that point. From where we stood it looked okay.

"Take it easy and go one at a time," the coach said, adjusting his goggles one last time before setting off. He had barely gone before the rest of the group nearly dived in after him to follow. I was certain that Carl would be the first and sure enough, off he went right after the coach, the stance on his skis still awkward, bow-legged and precarious. Three of them, all in a row, went schussing in one way or another after the coach. That left Carol, Scott, and me to look at them and then look at each other; and then I looked out at the mountains one more time before sending the others off and then going myself. Carol's pointing and near screaming sent a shock through me.

"Oh my G-!" and her words trailed off as I watched the last of that group fall and tumble and drop off into a gap in the snow at the bottom of the saddle. The gap was widening as we looked down from above. For a moment I was hoping that they had all skied past it and gone on to the other side to the north face and soon we would all be skiing powder. But somehow a crevasse had formed right along the narrow point of the saddle and they had all skied right into it, falling off the edge as it formed beneath them into an abyss. Then they were gone and we could hear their shouts and screams cutting across the thin quiet early morning mountain air.

"They've all fallen into it! Oh migod!" Carol screamed again and clenched herself against me. She felt hot and her soft body was trembling. I wanted to squeeze her out of my own fear but knew I had to act. The rescue was going to be up to us. Just like that.

"We'll ski down slowly. Try to stay to the far right, just along the rocks. Stop way above the crack and don't go near." I tried to say it calmly but I was shaking.

"Do you think we should go for help?" Scott asked nervously.

"Depends on if anybody is injured."

"Are we ever going to get them out?" Carol asked.

"We're gonna try," I said and slowly, nervously, set out with the coil of rope feeling heavy over my shoulder and the snow feeling hard under my skis. I made slow meandering turns, not thinking about making good turns but wanting to make safe ones. My knees felt weak from the nerves and I had to put the bad thoughts out of my head. I could hear the others following, the sound of their skis crunching on the hard snow.

When I got to the bottom of the saddle I slowed up and made cautious turns and stayed close to the right side edge. I could look right down the rocky jagged slope right to where it came up to the snow. That's where I stopped and began taking my skis off. The other two were coming in behind me and did the same. I was starting to uncoil the rope and I could hear shouts of desperation coming from the edge of the precipice.

"Hang on!" I shouted but wasn't sure if they could hear me.

"What are you going to do?" Carol pleaded.

I tied the rope around my waist using a half hitch. I didn't know any fancy climbing knots so did what I knew would be secure. Then I looked at Carol and Scott and tried to be calm.

"Try to dig yourselves in here along the edge of the snow. Scott, you tie this end of the rope around your waist. Feed the rope out to me as I move over to them. If I pull on the rope or you see me going in, yank me back!" I exclaimed and knew I was talking too fast and had to slow down and felt sweat running off me.

"Do you think it will work? Like shouldn't we go for help?" Carol begged.

"Lars knows what he's doing, Carol. We've just got to stay back here and hold on." He turned to me and began to flex his stocky muscular body and said, "Just like a tug of war, right buddy?" We both smiled at each other and somehow felt confident we could help them even though we hadn't even seen them yet.

"Oh Lars, be careful," she said sweetly and I thought that was the nicest thing a girl had ever said to me. But now I had to be moving out.

I walked fast, my ski boots at first clomping on the hard snow that became softer underfoot as I approached the edge. I lay down on my stomach and moved the knot around my belly so that it was in the middle of my back. I looked back at Scott and Carol. They were sitting down now against the edge of the snow, ski boots dug in, dishing out the rope and nodding back to me. Scott gave me a thumbs-up and I started crawling towards the edge. The sun was now feeling hot on the back of my neck but the snow on my belly cool and I could feel my heart pounding as I came to the edge carefully, not knowing what to expect to see when I looked over.

Somehow everything felt quite normal and I put my head over the edge and looked down. There about ten to fifteen feet down in a small darkened room of snow were the rest of our group. They were all in a jumble and all had their skis off and were standing together and looked up at me and shouted my name in unison after I said, "Hey, anybody wanting a lift?"

Carl was the first to plead: "Get us out of here!" and the coach just looked up and smiled at me. The others all looked pretty anxious and Carl began pleading again.

"Shut up, Brock," the coach said quietly. He then spoke up to me: "How's it look up there, Svensson?"

I looked around at the edge of the crevasse. It ran for about 30 feet and then narrowed out to nothing. A thin bridge of snow must have covered it. The bridge had collapsed when they skied over it. The others just went right off the edge like lemmings behind him. I looked down into the dark abyss where they all stood—some white, some tanned and some red faces with those raccoon eyes from the wearing of goggles in the Colorado sunshine.

"Looks pretty safe here, coach. I think we can get you out of there. I've got Carol and Scott holding onto the other end of this. Is everybody all right down there?"

"Course we're all right, Svensson. Just a bit of hurt pride for some." The coach looked around at the others and gave Carl a stern stare.

"C'mon Svensson, get us out of here before it gets worse!" Carl pleaded again.

"Guess we'd better not keep you waiting then," I said and began to untie the knot and started to lower the rope down.

"We'll start with the lightest ones first," the coach said casually. "Then the skis, then me I guess." He took the end of the rope and began to tie it around Larry's waist. Larry hadn't said anything yet but looked up at me and smiled and finally said, "Don't drop me, Lars."

"Just hold on tight and climb out steady," I said down to him. Then I crawled back a bit from the edge and stood up and shouted back to the others who were standing now, Scott still holding onto the rope.

"They're all okay!" I shouted.

When I saw the relieved look on Carol's face turn into a smile I told them how we were going to pull them out. Scott dug himself back in like it was fourth down play at the goal line and pulled the rope taunt. I crawled back to the edge where I could see the rope digging into the snow. I took my green and white Grayrock team windbreaker off and slid it under the rope where it bit into the snow. Then I looked over the edge and saw Larry ready to climb out and the others standing anxiously beside him. I waved a hand back to the others and watched Larry begin his ascent out of the crevasse. He scrambled and the ones down in the abyss attempted to help by pushing from behind and snow slid off the wall of the crevasse as he slowly climbed upwards. I looked back to see Scott and Carol straining to hold the weight so I crawled back and dug the heels of my boots into the snow and assisted in the pulling on that rope and soon saw Larry's head sticking up above the edge of the snow. It would be easy from here on in and I knew it. I walked back to the edge and offered a hand and helped him out the last steps, then began to untie the knot around his waist. I told him to go and help pull with the others and all Larry could do was smile and pat me on the back before walking off. I lowered the rope back down again for the next one.

With Larry helping to pull the next one out was a little easier. Tom was next and he made pretty easy work of it as he had been climbing before. That only left two down in the crevasse: The Coach and Carl. When I sent the rope down for them they had already decided to send the gear up next. I watched them down in the dark abyss lashing the rope around a bundle of skis and poles. That was easy to pull out and coach called up to me and said to drag it all the way to where everybody was stationed. While Larry and Scott untied the bundle I looked down at the Coach and Carl. The Coach had a smile on his face but Carl still looked anxious.

"We'll get you out of there next," I called down to Carl.

"I've had enough of being down in this hole. Let's get a move on."

"Just relax, Carl—it's your turn now," the Coach said sternly. "Don't hurry. Take it easy. You'll be out in no time."

I was kinda glad to see the coach giving him a telling off while at the same time I knew he was trying to give him encouragement.

Larry came back with the rope and we lowered it down and the coach helped tie Carl up and I gave the signal to start pulling when he was ready. Carl stumbled a few times on his climb out and looked nervous until he was right at the lip. I offered him my hand but he didn't want to take it. He was scrambling to get out and kicking snow down at the coach and not making progress, so I decided to grab him by the shoulders, one hand on either side of his tanned face with its chiseled features and nice teeth not smiling now. He continued to scramble, trying to get out and finally made it. We ended up having a struggle like we were wrestling and I didn't like it.

He was standing up now and I tried to help him untie the rope but he pushed my arms away and said, "Don't ever try that again." He undid the knot and took the rope and began passing it back down into the crevasse. We watched the coach tie himself on and nonchalantly nod back up to us. Carl began to signal to the others but they all waited until I waved at them and then they began to pull.

I could tell the coach was going to be a tough pull so I suggested to Carl, "Why don't you go help pull?"

"Why don't you? I don't need some punk telling me what to do."

I felt bad about how Carl was behaving but didn't want to see the others struggling trying to get the coach out so I strode back a few steps and dug my ski boots into the snow and grabbed the tight line. I looked back and saw all the others pulling until they were red in the face. Scott smiled at me as he was at the end of the rope with it tied around his waist and he was now moving backwards which meant we were winning this tug of war with the coach and gravity. Carl just stood at the edge of the precipice and watched and soon we saw the coach's head emerge over the precipice. Carl of course helped him out and we all cheered and I felt better, almost as though I was going to cry.

I was so happy and relieved just sitting there on the snow at the top of the Professor. I closed my eyes for a moment and said a little prayer and felt like it changed everything; and I felt I had changed and felt taller when I got up and walked back towards the others who were beginning to put their skis on. It was like the job was over and we could ski down the Professor now.

Carol wasn't putting her skis on. I watched her running towards me and then I couldn't believe she was hugging me and squeezing me and kissed me on the cheek. She felt all warm and soft and it was just like doing a slow dance with a girl after doing some fast dances, yet better than that. She pulled away and her sunglasses were up on her head and those bright eyes still dazzled even though they were full of tears.

"You're some kind of a hero now, Lars"

"Not really."

"Yes you are! And I like heroes. I'd like to see you, be with you."

"Gosh Carol."

"I mean it. I'm looking forward to riding back home with you. We'll have lots to talk about, you and me."

"Let's get down this mountain first." I smiled and thought about the summer ahead and wasn't worried about working at the Mart with those Roscommon girls in their yellow blouses and white trousers and wondered how I would get time off to drive up to Gaylord.

The Coach and Carl walked past us. The Coach was coiling the rope and Carl was feeding it to him. Carl gave me and Carol a strange glare and the coach just nodded.

"Good job, Svensson. Get your skis on. You too, Carol. Everybody's gonna be wondering what's keeping us."

❧   ❧   ❧

Down in the parking everybody's patience was starting to wear. It was the final day of this skiing trip. The lifts were now running, at least the two chairs that paralleled each other up the steep face of International. A few of the parents were asking each other if anything had happened but Mr Brock was being a steady influence and telling everyone not to worry and they'd be there soon but they still asked what would they do if there had been an accident. Other cars full of skiers were pulling into the parking lot above 10,000 feet and looking up at the top of the Professor, realizing that everybody was waiting to watch a group of skiers coming down to a big reception.

Jim Head removed his sunglasses so he could look at Judy Binns. Judy had her goggles resting around her neck and was facing the morning sun with her eyes closed, trying to blend out a bit of her raccoon eyes.

"Aren't you gonna watch Lars come down, Judy?" he asked, trying to get her attention.

"Why would I want to be watching Lars?" she stated without opening her eyes.

"Everybody seems to think you two have something going."

"That's a joke. There's nothing between us." She thought about skiing with Lars at various times during the week and looking him in the eyes whenever they rode up the lift together. She liked looking into those blue eyes when he had his sunglasses off, even if the whites were bloodshot from the sun. Part of her was hoping he would ask her out and part of her didn't want to get involved. He never did ask her and now Jim's suggestion didn't surprise her.

"Maybe we should go skiing then."

"Yeah, maybe we should," she said and looked at Jim with his acne-covered face and she thought to herself maybe Jim would be better for her anyhow. He certainly was richer. She gave him a smile and just before she could say, "let's go," someone in the group of fifty or so people shouted: "Look, there they are!"

Everyone started to point towards plumes of snow rising from the distant shapes of skiers up at the summit beginning to make turns in the snow.

The Toboggan Run

*L*ars usually had dinner by himself after practice. It would be waiting in the oven when he came in. Tonight the rest of the family were trooping between the dining room and the kitchen, cleaning plates and stacking them in the kitchen sink and making themselves scarce, barely looking at him but sticking around long enough to see him. He was glad his dad was out of town, otherwise there might be real trouble. His younger brother Fritz was searching through the refrigerator and he turned towards Lars holding the last big slice of blueberry pie still in the heavy pie tin. He forced a smile showing a few missing teeth.

"How was practice?" Fritz shouted across the kitchen.

"Okay—we ran a gs," Lars answered quietly, setting his car keys on the counter by the door while taking his coat and boots off.

"How's Judy?"

"What's it to you?"

"Does she still want your body?"

Before Lars could take a step his mother turned around from the hot stove and glared at both of them. She held his dinner on a plate, covered in aluminum foil. Her plump face was flushed with anger.

"Shuddap, Fritz! She's already caused enough trouble."

Fritz didn't even look at his mother. He just took the pie tin with him and headed for the TV room where all the other brothers and sisters had gone. Lars had no idea what was on TV right now, probably the last of *Johnny Quest* before the news. There was no watching television while eating dinner in the Svensson household, no matter how late somebody came home. He sat on his own at the big table with its white Formica top glaring in the light and waited for his mother to start. The steaming plate heaped full of mashed potatoes, pork chops and peas was set in front of him with the expected crash of china on Formica.

"Here, eat this and then do the dishes before you do anything else," she said, forcing the words out at him. She walked over towards the door leading out to the garage and picked up the afternoon copy of the *Bay City Times* lying on the counter with the other clutter of school bags, purses, keys and books. Lars began eating the dry hot food while his mother pretended to read the paper.

"By the way, we know all about it. Her mother called this afternoon. You're to stay away from that tramp." She turned the pages past articles on President Ford and the energy crisis, ruffling the sheets of newsprint and letting the words hang in the air. Just as she began to head towards the living room with the paper now folded under her arm she picked up his ring of keys off the counter to look at them. "I'm taking your car keys away until your father gets home. This is a disgrace." His mother of seventeen years dropped the keys into the pocket of a dirty apron and walked away.

Lars sat quietly and took his time eating dinner. He wanted to think about better times—like out at the lake last summer when they agreed to start this seriously. He was amazed how it somehow kept going through the fall with him playing football while Judy playing on the first-ever girls' basketball team at Grayrock. They managed to find time for each other, mostly when he took her home from practice in his car with her hair still wet and fresh from a shower. Just as soon as fall sports were over he would pick her up early in the morning with his car to go to dryland training at the high school gym. Winter came and it was still going strong and he thought about all the practicing and running gates in the bowl at Bear Mountain after school and laughing together while riding up the hill on the T-Bar. It was all so good for him and now it seemed like it was all over.

He ate the last of the food finishing the last pork chop right down to the bone. Then he rose from his chair and brought his plate and the last remaining items on the table over to the sink. After tossing the bones in the trash can he set the plate in the sink with all the other dishes and it upset the balance of the pile and caused a crash. He walked back towards the living room and stood in the archway looking at his mother still pretending to read the paper. He looked out the big picture window at the snow on the lawn and the hedge and further out to the snow banks lining M-93. It would be getting dark soon.

"How am I going to get to work?" he asked loud enough to gain attention. His mother responded in the same tone.

"That's your problem. Besides, you're not working tonight."

He paused for a moment and chose his words, carefully, quietly.

"I didn't want it to happen this way mom, honest.

"That's the way it always happens and you'd better learn that right away," came the response as she set the paper down and glared at him. "Her parents wanted her to have a future. We wanted you to have a future. Now look at what you've done."

"Don't you think this is something for me to straighten out? "

"The hell with you! You've ruined her. Now just leave her alone."

With that Mrs Svensson returned to the newspaper, deliberately ruffling the pages to announce that all discussion was over with. He just looked at her and shrugged his shoulders and ran his hands through his thick blond hair and looked out the window at the snow. He went back into the kitchen.

He went to the refrigerator and pulled open the big white metal door. He was greeted by the glare of the white light and the hum of the electric motor kicking in. There was a tub of cottage cheese and maybe he'd have some of that for dessert as Fritz had taken the last of the pie. He didn't deserve to have pie. He grabbed a spoon and tried a mouthful. It was first nice and cold but then the sour taste came through and he spat it out into the trashcan and dumped the tub into the trash too. Then he hurled the spoon into the sink and it clanged off the plates and back onto the floor. He told himself to stop it right there and took a deep breath and let it out and began piling the dishes out of the sink and running the water until it got hot. He squirted some of that Spartan brand liquid soap into the steaming water running from the tap and realized his hands were shaking. He moved the tap over to the rinsing sink and began piling the dirty dishes into the soapy water and thought about her. He spoke to himself in short sentences and then let his thoughts about her take over.

Maybe she'll be there tonight. Maybe we can figure something out. Gosh, her parents have enough money; maybe we could just go away together. We want to be together. She told me that just last week on Valentine's Day. She even said she loved me when I gave her the flowers and I felt so good about it. And now all this. It should be better than this. Like it was out in Colorado last spring and on the beach at the lake last summer. I loved the smell of the Coppertone on her skin. I'll never forget being alone together down by the cabin below tree line at A-Basin, our lips touching for the first time. Then that long ride back to Michigan, sitting together in the back of that big Ford van, just looking into each other's eyes and then finding the nerve to touch and feel, reluctantly at first and then as a matter of course. And our summer at the lake, more Coppertone and water skiing with Toots on days off with his girlfriend and Judy in her pink bikini tight on that body and nights after work in the dark on that quiet beach with just a fire to sit beside on a blanket sometimes staying there all night.

"Still dreaming about her?" came the voice of his older sister Greta, her long blonde hair still wet after a shower and her thin fit body in a soft green sweat suit. Lars looked at her and shrugged his shoulders.

"You know, maybe you ought to say something to her," she said. "I'll bet she'll be skiing tonight. I heard some of the girls talking."

"What were they saying?"

"I think you better find that out from her. Look, I'd give you a ride but Tom is coming by for me. We have to study for a Government Test."

"Yeah, I'm sure, sis. On a Friday night?"

"Hey, the basketball team is away and there's no dance, so what's a girl gonna do?"

"I'll leave it to your imagination. Discuss Amendments to the Bill of Rights?"

Greta smiled at him and winked, then leaned against the archway leading from that cluttered kitchen with no windows to the TV room. She was always able to handle herself and would never get into this kind of a mess.

"Look, you might as well finish those dishes, then ski over. There's still plenty of light and besides, there's a full moon tonight."

"You're right. I'll see her. Toots will probably be there anyhow and we'll get some practice in, too. I'll be able to get a ride home from him."

"Is practicing all you guys can think about?"

"That's all I've got. You know its over now."

"Nothing is over with. You've got to speak to her."

"What about mom?"

"I'll take care of mom."

"You're too good to me."

"That's what big sisters are for sometimes." She walked past him and patted him on the butt and headed towards the living room. She turned to look back at him, smiling just like he would see her doing to the boys in the hallways of Grayrock High School whenever she wore a short skirt. But tonight she was in sweats and she pointed to the garage door and then walked around the corner.

Lars worked quickly to finish the dishes, leaving them to drain in the rack beside the rinsing sink. He rinsed the dishcloth and rang it out and went over to the kitchen table and wiped off the big Formica surface. When the tabletop was glistening he turned towards the kitchen sink and tossed the dishcloth as though it were a basketball shot and it landed in the sink from fifteen feet away and he felt good. His Sorel boots were sitting beside the garage door and he slipped them on and then quietly opened the door and walked into the cooler air of the garage and out towards his car sitting on the hard packed snow of the driveway.

The ski boots were in the back of the Chevy Vega Hatchback, as was the rest of his gear. The vinyl seat cracked and crinkled when he sat down to change into the battered pair of Nordicas. He hadn't changed out of his ski pants and he was ready to go after loosely buckling the boots. He pulled the tight fitting racing shell coat on and began taking the skis off the roof rack. He noticed the rack had rubbed into the lime green paint and thought maybe he ought to touch that up at the end of the season. Then again, maybe not. The Vega wasn't much of a car but it was his, bought with the money he saved working at The Mart with all those cute girls from Roscommon who wanted him but he stayed away from them because he had Judy. He stood there with his skis over his shoulder and poles together in his hand and looked at this car and looked at the humble farmhouse and thought he had nothing unless he had Judy. He set off towards the path through the snow leading around the back towards the wood pole barn. A few hundred feet beyond that was the grade of the Military Road and the snow beneath was hard and easy to walk on.

Michigan number 93 was a wide beautiful highway that was purpose-built to run from M-72 to the military base on the far shore of

Lake Margaret. It went past the front of the Svensson's farm and replaced the Military Road, which was now deserted and ran behind the farm. In the summer it was nothing but a dirt track that Lars and his friends used to ride their bikes on. It the winter it was a snowmobile trail and the most direct route to the ski hill. Lars had used it all the time until he could drive and it seemed like old times again tonight. The surface was hard from the track left by the snowmobiles and he set the Volkl Sapporos down and stepped in the bindings. He secured the safety straps loosely and grabbed his poles and began pushing along the flat track, easily picking up speed as his skis clicked along over the tiny ridges left by the snowmobiles. The light was still good and he looked into the woods lining both sides of the road to see the leafless oak trees poking out of the carpet of white. Evening was coming and the trees looked so lonely with no wind to play with the branches.

After about a mile the road came to a clearing. This was the outrun from the Toboggan Ride at Bear Mountain. The road was meant to curve right around the big expanse of flat ground about the size of a football field. But everyone took the short cut straight across the end of the run, including the snowmobiles. There was a rope barrier and an arrow on a fencepost to direct everyone around the outrun. The rope was strung so high up that the snowmobiles could pass underneath without stopping and Lars did the same. He began to skate across the clearing. It was slightly uphill but then leveled out again when it met the centerline of the toboggan run. Lars stopped there and looked up the run cut straight up through the trees.

The Toboggan run was famous. People came by the busload to experience the speed and thrills of being together during winter in Michigan. There was a big brick building at the top of the run where they took the toboggans and crowds by the truck full along a trail winding around the back of the hill. Inside the building there were two boarding stations that sent the riders in the ten-foot long wood toboggans hurtling down the parallel channels straight to the bottom. The channels were dug into the ground about eight inches, lined with thick rounded rusty red metal on the sides. Solid ice formed the running surface. Groups would sometimes come to race each other and there would be lots of shouting and drinking by the crowds that gathered at the outrun. Lars used to stop and watch on his way over to the hill on Saturdays before he started working and driving and was amazed how fast they went and how it would be over in a few seconds. Advertisements in the *Bay City Times* said you could go as fast as 125 miles per hour. Nobody living locally thought it was that fast and Lars thought the $2.00 per ride was a lot especially when you could ski a whole season at Bear Mountain for $36.

He looked across from the start of the toboggan run to the top of the ski runs and saw the mercury lights starting to glow softly and began skating towards the lodge. It wasn't far now and slightly downhill once off the outrun and on the service road to the hill that split away from the Military Road.

There were a few other people arriving by car just as he reached the lodge. Most of them were regulars, parents dropping off their kids for a Friday night of fun. The skis were left in the wooden racks on the slope-facing side of the lodge while they all went inside to collect lift tickets. Lars rarely bothered to go in and sign the book and collect a ticket as the lift attendants knew him well and didn't bother to check tickets very often. He skied straight over to the T-bar and began riding up.

The snow felt firm underneath but not icy. It would be different in a few weeks when it started to warm up, the snow turning slushy in the day and then freezing at night. But now it was nice and Lars watched the moon rising up through the trees and over the horizon as he traveled up the hill. When he reached the summit he released the T-bar and watched it retract slowly on the hydraulic cylinder. The cable traveling around the pulleys on the lift towers made a steady plug-plug sound. He was the first person up the hill and there were no other sounds and he went to the crest of the hill. Lars looked

out at the moon rising over the jack pine and oak forest running out
to the horizon, now darkening into the distance. He saw lights moving on the thin lines cut through the trees which were the roads leading to Grayrock where scattered lights were coming on in the town.

He made several runs down the Bowl, practicing his turns in a
straight descent of the fall line. He liked to warm up this way, making
as many turns as possible in a run. It was just back and forth, driving
his knees as hard as he could into each turn. He kept his shoulders
square and pointing down the hill and his rhythm ticked like a pendulum. After each run he would ride up the T-bar and look at the
other skiers now out on the hill and look behind him down to the
bottom to see who was arriving.

He saw Judy Binns stepping outside the lodge with three other
people. One looked like Jane who was her best friend and used to be
Toots' girlfriend. He didn't recognize the two other boys who looked
like they were showing the girls their skis. Lars let the T-bar out from
underneath him and watched it swing from side to side as it
retracted. He skied down quickly, not concentrating on his turns but
watching them all putting their skis on. When he got to the bottom
the other three had left for the lift, leaving Judy standing on her own
by the ski racks. Jane nodded at Lars as he passed quickly and he
nodded back and looked at the boys but still didn't recognize them.

He was looking at Judy. She looked healthy, wearing those green
ski pants and a blue sweater, silky blonde hair in a ponytail poking
out beneath a green wool hat. The hair rested on the back of her
shoulder in a gentle curve. The off red-lipstick was new and somehow made her look older. The rest of her face was as young and fresh
as it ever was and everything seemed fine and he was with her now.

"Who are they?" he asked when he stopped beside her. He wanted
to kiss her and hold her but knew it was not the right thing to do, not
right now.

"Some guys we know from downstate. They ski for Bloomfield
Hills." She smiled at him, standing straight on her skis. He could

smell that lemony perfume she always liked. He liked it too and moved closer to her. She began moving across the snow towards the lift and spoke to him again.

"They wanted to know if they could run some gates with us tonight."

"Sure," Lars replied, just looking at her, pushing his skis along with his poles. "I was going to wait until Toots came. Thought we'd practice a few hand drills."

"I'm going to ski with them until you guys set a course. Let's go. I want to catch up to them." She began skating across the snow at the bottom flats towards the lift station. It seemed to Lars as if nothing was the matter and they got on the T-bar and began riding up and neither said anything for a while. Their skis ran through the grooves cut in the snow for the T-bar track. They watched other people skiing and he felt he had to say something soon.

"Look, I…"

"Don't say anything. Can't you see it's all over?" Judy interrupted him, looking down at the snow. Her voice sounded on the verge of breaking. Lars put his arm around her.

"I'll take care of you. It'll be okay."

"No it won't. It can't be."

"I want it to be good for us. We have a good thing going." He tried to squeeze her with the arm around her as they rode up the lift. She kept looking down and was bent over slightly and he could feel her trembling. She straightened up and looked at him with tears welling in her eyes.

"It never started," she said tensely. "If you don't realize that, you're stupid." She took her glove off and reached behind her to pull a tissue out of her back hip pocket to wipe her face. He let her take her time to pull herself together.

"How far gone are you?"

"Two months, Lars."

"What will you do, Judy?"

"None of your business. It's my problem."

"No, it's our problem."

"I need to take care of this on my own. I'm sorry Lars. I'll need to go away."

"I'll go with you."

"No you won't," she said like she meant it.

They didn't say anything until they reached the top of the hill. Jane and the two boys were waiting at the top of the Bowl, watching Lars and Judy getting off the T-bar. They stopped on the flat summit and Judy turned to him, her eyes reaching out like she wanted to say something. Lars took his goggles off to look into her eyes.

"I'm not angry with you," she said.

"I'm so sorry all of this happened."

"It's not your fault."

"What's that supposed to mean? I'm a part of this, too."

"I don't want to go into this, Lars. Not now."

He paused. "I understand. You want me to come over and say hi to your friends?"

"No. Not yet. Why don't you go set a course? We'll come over in awhile."

"You're okay then?"

"Yeah. I've got to go be a big girl now." She forced a smile at him and he smiled back and he watched her ski away.

Lars turned to cross over the T-bar line and head down the slope they called Number One. By the time he had skied down to the copse of oak trees where they kept the bamboo poles in a barrel, tears were welling up in his eyes. He put the goggles back on again and the light seemed strange and nothing had any color for a while, just a yellow tint. He pulled the wrist straps off and tossed the ski poles down onto the snow and grabbed the heavy metal spud and about ten bamboo poles and slid down to a pitch of the slope that had a flat crest and could serve as a starting gate.

The setting of the course didn't matter much to him. Nothing mattered much to him right now. He made a starting gate with two poles and then slid down about thirty feet to set the first gate. That was a long way from the start and would let them pick up some good speed. He set a straight line of poles after that, closely spaced to make you turn quick and keep up your speed from the start. Some people called it a "hand drill" because it forced you to keep your hands in front and avoid big pole-plants. It made you go fast and be quick on your skis. It also meant you would hit the bamboo with your knees and shoulders as you passed each pole. Lars wanted to hit something right now. It would make him feel better.

Just as he was finishing he saw Toots riding up the T-bar. He waved and Toots shouted over to him.

"Let's set a dual!"

"You'll need to get some more poles!" Lars shouted back.

"Bring the spud back up!"

"Okay." Lars waved and began sidestepping back up through the course. He tried to visualize his way down through the line of poles, making a right turn on the first pole and then through each turn down to the finish where he stood. That determined which side of each pole he would step through on his way back to the start. Sidestepping up would flatten out any loose snow. As he climbed past each pole he checked it to see it was well into the snow. The spud had made good holes through the hard snow and the poles were each inserted about two feet into the snow. They were not going to come out of the snow when you hit them tonight, unless you hooked a tip or something and crashed. Lars made it to the start and felt warm from the climb.

He looked across to the Bowl and saw Judy and Jane skiing down following those downstate guys. The girls were making better turns than the downstate boys. Lars watched them ski down to the bottom and stop and chat to each other and he could tell they were laughing and having fun together. He saw Toots coming down towards him now, carrying a bundle of poles over one shoulder and holding his ski poles in the other hand. He stopped alongside Lars and placed the ski poles into the snow.

"You ready for some racing?"

"Sure"

"That looks tight enough, what you've set there."

"We ought to be going pretty fast by the first gate."

"Here, you take the poles and I'll get the spud." Toots handed Lars the bundle, taking one of the ten-foot long lengths of bamboo from him. He laid the pole on the snow and used it to measure out a two-length gap between the two courses. After making an identical starting gate he slid down to where he was parallel to the first gate and Lars followed him. Once again he took the time to measure out the correct gap and kept eyeing Lars' course to see that the two were as even as they could be. Lars looked across and saw Judy riding up the T-bar with one of those downstate guys. They must have stayed at the bottom a long time talking and laughing. He thought nothing of it because he was now setting a short dual slalom with his friend Toots and soon he would be practicing.

"I think we're ready," Toots said as he set the final bamboo pole into the snow.

"Looks pretty good," Lars replied as he looked up the parallel lines of poles running down the pitch.

"We could always walk up. It'll be quicker."

"Maybe next run. Besides, my poles are up at the barrel."

"Let's get at it then," Toots announced as he picked up the spud and headed off. Lars followed him towards the lift station, not making any turns.

Nothing was said for a while as they rode up the T-bar together. Lars just watched their shadows on the snow made by the mercury lights atop the lift towers. The shadows changed as they rode up the hill, passing one tower and then the shadow shifting like a sundial on a fast speed film as they approached another.

"It's better if its over, Lars."

"I don't want it to be over," Lars said, still looking at the shadows.

"C'mon, man. There's no future with her."

"I'll be the judge of that."

"Fine. But think about your future. It'll be better without her."

"I really thought we had it together. I just feel so empty, so darn helpless."

"There will be others, Lars. Just like there will be other races. It will get better."

"What about her condition? I just can't leave her."

"I wouldn't worry about that. It might not even be yours."

"What's that supposed to mean!" Lars heard himself shouting and he looked up at Toots and then scanned the hill to see Judy still skiing in the Bowl with her friends.

"She's been two-timing you, man. It's those downstate guys. I saw her and Jane hanging out with them last summer out at the lake. Why do you think I've finished with Jane?"

"I can't believe you're saying this. Judy isn't like that."

"You wanna bet? I've seen 'em skiing together at the weekends when you've been working. I'd just leave her to it and forget about it." Toots spoke quietly as though he were offering confidential advice, like one of those stockbrokers in a TV advert.

Lars felt a burning inside him at first, his skin all hot even on a winter night. Then he felt sorrow as he thought about the exciting and happy times with Judy and all the things they did. But there were also the other times when she wasn't as interested as he'd like her to be. So this was it. It really was over. Maybe it never started. Tears began to gel in his eyes. He fought the feeling and gripped his fists tightly around the ski poles. He looked down for the last time at the small shadows on the tips of his skis change from the right side to the left side as they approached the last lift tower at the summit of Bear Mountain.

After retrieving his poles from the barrel by the copse of leafless oak trees, Lars followed Toots down to the start of the course. They lined up together in the respective starting gates, Toots already in the course he had set and Lars taking up a position in the other. They both readied themselves by propping their ski poles in front of the start gate and crouched low behind it, ready to spring out with an explosive start and pick up speed before the first gate. Lars looked down the pitch. It seemed a long way before the first gate and steep enough to pick up real speed. For a moment he thought about the teenagers in their fast cars in California in that movie, getting ready for a drag race that would take them to the edge of a cliff and he barely heard Toots' command:

"On my word, Lars. Racers ready."

"Born ready," Lars replied and crouched down further.

"Three, two, one, go!" Toots shouted and they were both off together, leaping out of the start and making short skating steps on their skis, pushing hard towards the first gate. Lars felt like he had tremendous energy and was ahead at the first turn, puffing hard, preparing to make quick turns and strike the bamboo poles. First gate, *wham, smack,* right into his shoulder, then quickly past the second gate and skis running fast and turning quick and in the lead and then losing his balance on a turn somewhere in the middle and having to recover and keep his speed up. Toots streamed past, slapping his shoulders on each pole, hands in tight to his body, skis running fast and letting gravity and quick turns take him ahead and beat Lars to the finish by half a gate length. They both rammed their skis into the snow, Toots to the left and Lars to the right. Each sent a huge rooster tail of snow flying.

"Hey, you almost had me there!" Toots shouted across to Lars. He was the top racer on the Grayrock team and for good reason. Lars wasn't far behind him in most races and while trying to catch his breath replied back, "Felt pretty good! 'Cept for that third gate. I really had to crank to stay in it."

They both began sidestepping up and through their courses, resetting the poles that were bent over from striking them on the way down. Lars' shoulders felt bruised already and his left knee was feeling pain from striking a gate. But he wasn't going to say anything about it, this was ski racing and just like football it was a contact sport and he loved it all when it felt good. By the time they reached the starting gates and were ready to swap courses for another run they noticed Judy and Jane coming down from the top of the Number One, followed by the downstate guys. Lars watched them all making their turns and he liked the way Judy stood on her skis, knees bent, unweighting, pole planting, turning. The downstate guys looked clumsy, sliding out of their turns.

"Looks like we've got some turkeys here tonight," Toots said, looking up at them and then looking over to Lars. "If they try to get smart I'll handle them."

"I can handle myself," Lars replied.

So there were six of them at the starting gates. Lars looked at the downstate guys in their new Ellese ski pants and matching padded sweaters. They had dark goggles on so he could not see their eyes. They were both about the same size as Lars but probably Seniors judging from the stubble on their faces.

"What kind of a course is this?" one of them asked in a deep voice.

"It's just a bit of dual slalom," Toots replied. "Have a go. Or would you care to race against one of us?"

"Those gates should have at least a five-meter radius," the other said, standing beside Judy. His voice sounded a bit weak and squeaky.

"We couldn't give a damn about that. You guys wanna race or just talk? We let our skis do the talkin' around here," Lars said in a stern reply, feeling his face getting hot.

"Lars, that's not very nice," Jane said. She looked at Toots but he looked away, staring at Judy.

"Maybe you girls ought to go first," Toots said. "The course needs slipping."

"Ha-ha. Very funny, Toots," Jane replied. The two of them would not look at each other. Lars on the other hand could do nothing but look at Judy.

"Yeah, why don't you ladies go first. We're all gentlemen here, aren't we?" one of the downstate guys said while adjusting his goggles like the racers did on TV before a run.

"All right, if you insist then," Judy said with a smile back towards him and she slid over to one of the starting gates.

Lars felt his face getting hotter as the downstate guy watched her bending over in the starting gate. Jane took to the other course and Toots counted them off. They both made slow starts and didn't push at all to the first gate and Jane made a bit of a check turn to slow down but then went through the course fine without touching any poles. Judy made good turns through her course and finished a full gate length ahead of Jane.

"Not bad. Those girls ski real well. Do you help them out in practice?" The other downstate guy spoke in his funny voice.

"Yeah, we're all gentlemen around here," Toots replied. "Let's not hang around." Then he asked in a friendly way: "What's your name?"

"Joe—Joe Demp," the taller one with the deep voice replied. "This here is Chuck." Neither offered to shake hands and Lars wasn't going to offer.

"You guys ski for Bloomfield Hills?"

"Yeah," came the reply in unison.

"Hey Lars, we won't have much trouble in Regionals this year, will we?"

"Not by what I've seen so far," Lars replied. That didn't raise a response so Toots waved a ski pole and spoke.

"Hey Joe, choose a course. I'm going to kick your ass."

The one called Joe took a gulp and slid over to the course Lars had set. Toots went to his starting gate. Lars counted them off and Toots stormed out of the gate and blazed his way through to the first gate. Joe tripped over his ski pole at the start and then pushed hard to catch up and had good speed but went wide on the first turn, then hooked the tip of his ski on the second pole and cart-wheeled down the pitch through the gates, snow and equipment flying and the course in a mess of twisted bamboo. Toots kept on skiing through to the finish and stopped next to the girls just as Judy screamed, "Oh migod!" The one called Joe lay on the snow for a few moments and then started moving after Toots shouted back up the pitch: "Hey, you all right!"

Lars and the one with the funny voice called Chuck skied down to the wreckage, picking up bamboo and ski poles along the way. Both skis had come off and Lars picked up one of the new Rossingnol skis with the Salomon bindings and those ski brakes that had just come out. Lars was standing just above Joe holding onto the ski, waiting for him to walk up.

"Serves you guys right, coming up here, trying to act cool. You can't even ski."

"You gonna make something of it?" Downstate Joe ran up the pitch towards Lars. He was burning hot now and ready to defend himself with Joe's ski if he needed to but Chuck slid in between them. Lars saw Toots sidestepping up the hill quickly. The girls were still standing down at the bottom of the course looking up.

"This isn't worth it, Joe," the squeaky voice suggested trying to put space between the two of them. Lars was ready even if he still had his skis on. "C'mon, get your skis on and we'll get the girls and get out of here."

"Yeah, you go do that," Lars said, thrusting the ski at Chuck who handed it over to Joe.

"Chuck, you know he's the one who's supposed to be with Judy."

"Yeah—I know," Chuck said looking down at the snow. "I guess we have something in common," he said, looking up at Lars, taking his goggles off.

Lars could look at the eyes now and they looked tired. He knew the whole story now and just nodded his head at the one called Chuck and he suddenly felt sorry for him. Toots had by now side-stepped up to where they were and wasn't breathing hard but had his goggles up on his forehead over his green Grayrock wool hat. Lars looked down at the girls still standing together at the end of the course. He looked out across beyond the Bowl at the full moon rising and heard Toots' voice.

"These guys causing you any trouble, Lars?"

"Naw, Toots. Just a bit of a 'yard sale' here, that's all."

The one called Chuck gave out a weak laugh and Joe joined in with: "You can say that again. We'll help you reset it."

"Don't worry about it. We're gonna pick it up, eh Toots?" Lars gave a nod to his friend. "I just wanna have a word with Judy. See you in a few minutes." He skied off down to where the girls were standing. They both just looked at him and he thought they didn't look so pretty any more.

"I bet you think you're really cool, two-timing us. I hope its been fun."

"How can you say that, Lars!" Jane exclaimed.

"Stay out of it, Jane. I want to have a word with Judy."

Judy looked at Jane and said to her, "I'll see you in the lodge, Jane. This won't take long." Jane slid away and they watched her and then looked up the hill. The downstate guys were helping Toots tear the course down.

"You guys had enough already?" Judy asked, flicking her ponytail back over her shoulder when she turned to look at Lars again. He didn't want to look at her but knew he had to say it all and not lose control even though he felt like it. He started with, "Yeah, we've just about had enough, Judy. I think you've hurt about enough people, including yourself. None of us are going to end up happy out of this. I've lost you. That guy up there has lost all his self-respect—I can see it a mile away."

"Maybe you never had me, Lars. I don't belong to anybody."

"Not anymore, that's for sure. Maybe never. Let's chalk this up to experience."

"I guess there's nothing more to say then, is there?"

"Other than I wish we had had the chance to do this all differently. Maybe being friends first would have made a difference." They looked into each other's eyes and somehow knew something good could come of this now.

"We can still be friends. I'll be back."

"Somehow I have my doubts," Lars said slyly and thought for a moment and looked over at the moon and smiled at her and said finally, "but I'll try."

Judy smiled back at him, flashing a few of those perfectly white teeth. She inched closer to him. "You know, we were all thinking of going tobogganing tomorrow."

"Are you okay for doing that? I mean…"

Judy touched his arm to interrupt him. "Of course I'll be okay. Those guys have to go south tomorrow night. We could all be friends, just have some fun."

"You know I have to work tomorrow, otherwise I'd come."

"Sure. Look, Jane and I will probably come skiing again tomorrow night. Think you can make it? I mean you and Toots? We'd have a good time."

"We'll see. I'll talk to Toots." Lars watched Toots ski past with all the bamboo poles over his shoulder heading for the lift. The down-state guys skied past and made their way towards the lodge.

"Guess its goodbye then," and she leaned over standing on one ski and gave him a quick kiss on his cheek. He liked that and he knew there would be lipstick on his cheek and he didn't care and he smelled the perfume and wanted to hug her but she turned to ski away. All he could say towards her was, "Take care of yourself, Judy."

Toots waited for Lars at the lift station and they rode up the T-bar together. Toots had brought down the spud and his ski poles with the bamboo. Lars took the spud and the ski poles. Toots had the bamboo over his shoulder nearest Lars so it blocked his face and he didn't say anything. Lars just looked up at the moon and down at the shadows. When they got to the top he told him about Jane and Judy just wanting to ski tomorrow night and asked if he could get a ride home tonight. Toots said he didn't know if he would come skiing or not as he was planning to ski during the day and his brothers were home from Central and they might want to run some gates. Lars said he would ski over anyhow after work and see what happened. They put the poles and spud away and skied down to Toots' car. On the way home they listened to the end of the basketball game. Grayrock was losing to Petoskey by about ten points in the third quarter and neither said much other than good night and thanks and see you later when Toots dropped Lars off on M-93 outside his house. Lars never mentioned the toboggan run.

On Saturday morning Lars called up his workmate Doug to get a ride into work. It meant he would have to go in a bit earlier as Doug opened up on a Saturday but that didn't matter. Doug was a Vietnam Veteran and lived alone in his parents' house out at the lake and drove an old Land Cruiser retrofitted with Bachman Overdrive. Doug would usually tell Lars stories about military life but never about Vietnam. Today Lars told him everything about Judy because that was the reason he wasn't driving his Vega. When Lars had finished letting out all his thoughts Doug scratched his beard and finished the conversation with, "Consider yourself lucky, man. I drive around this here town some nights so horny I could jump anything."

Lars had to laugh at that but it didn't help him much. He missed Judy already.

He spent the whole day at the Mart stocking shelves and cleaning out the freight room. It hadn't been done for weeks and was a big job. There were plenty of other people in to look after customers and he wanted to be alone and just do some work. He didn't even talk to the girls from Roscommon, other than saying hello and talking about basketball during coffee break. The word on him would be out soon, if they didn't know already. The boss was away today and soon enough he would hear about it and give Lars one of those fatherly-type lectures in the coffee lounge. Everyone in the town knew that Krosier had gotten a girl from Roscommon pregnant when he went to Grayrock high. His parents were so disgraced they sent him away to Boarding School and he never returned until a few years ago after earning his fortune and having enough money to build the Mart on what was the old golf course along the Business Loop. Lars didn't think that would happen to him because his parents could not afford Boarding School. What he did hope would happen was Judy would come skiing tonight and they would work this out.

One of the other floor managers had agreed to lock up so Doug and Lars headed home early. He was even home ahead of his mom and Greta who had gone together to Traverse City to go shopping. The only person in the house was Fritz who was watching ABC's *Wide World of Sports* on the TV. There was some World Cup skiing coming on later in the program but Lars knew it was taped and he had already seen the result in *Ski Racing*, another win for Ingemar Stenmark but both the Mahre brothers had made the top ten. He didn't want to stick around and listen to Fritz needle him about Judy so he got ready and headed off to Bear Mountain on his skis.

The weather had turned milder and he felt warm, almost sweaty when he reached the outrun of the toboggan run. There were several bits of toboggan lying in the snow at the outrun. He had not noted the debris the night before. Lars looked up the twin lines of metal-lined track leading up to the red brick building at the top. He bent down and picked up a piece of weathered laminated wood, a bit of varnish still on it. Just one of those old toboggans breaking up again, he thought. He had seen it all before. But he had never seen the bits of hard black plastic also lying in the snow. Maybe someone came down in a plastic toboggan and it broke up, too. He didn't notice the red patches on the snow a bit further away from the debris and he skied on towards Bear Mountain thinking about Judy being there tonight and what he would say to her to make her think differently.

It was starting to get dark by the time he reached the lodge. The mercury lights were warming up and illuminating the runs. The T-bar was running but hardly anybody was out skiing yet. Lars stopped to look inside the lodge on the chance that Judy and Jane might already be there but all he saw were a few kids and a few young parents taking them skiing on a Saturday night. While he had his skis off he walked through the cafeteria and smelled the cooking oil for the French fries and burgers that people would be having later. He used the toilets at the far end of the lodge and then went out to ski a few runs and wait for the girls to arrive.

He was coming down the Bowl working on his turns for about the fourth run of the night and still no sign of anybody. As he skied across the flat section and over the crest of the last headwall he saw a car pull into the parking lot right at the bottom of the run. It was Toots' Ford Maverick and he saw Toots getting out of the car and waving at him as he skied closer, still making good carved turns right down to the bottom. The snow felt good tonight. Toots was wearing blue jeans but he skied in jeans much of the time. He did not take his skis out of the car and the lights were still switched on.

Lars kept his speed up and skied right down to the car and stopped right in front of the single rail wood fence. He heard the engine of the Maverick idling.

"Hey Toots, you left your lights on."

"Nobody's told you. Get your skis off and get in the car. I'll take you to the hospital." Toots sounded anxious.

"What's happened? Tell me!"

"Judy and Jane. They went tobogganing with those downstate guys today." Before he could finish Lars pictured the bits of wood and plastic he had seen earlier and said "No!" to himself but tried to stay calm while Toots kept talking. He started taking his skis off.

"They hit a snowmobile taking a shortcut across the outrun. They're all at Mercy but one of 'em might be transferred to Saginaw by now. The snowmobiler's dead—heart attack."

"Can you take me to them?"

"Yeah, let's go. Get your skis into the car. Don't worry about your boots."

They placed everything into the car and Toots was reversing out before Lars had the door closed. He drove fast along the Bear Mountain access road and didn't stop at the junction with M-93. Neither said anything for a while until the engine had quieted down once they were doing seventy on the straight highway.

"How are they?" Lars finally asked. "Are they hurt bad?"

"I dunno, Lars. They're all pretty bad but I saw Dr Balma and he thought Jane and Judy were okay. Those two guys are pretty bad."

"Did you see anything?"

"I was out running gates with my brothers. Coach Wisner had come out too, just to say hi to Gerry and see how he was doing in college. They paged him to come to the Patrol Room and took him out to the outrun by snowmobile. I guess he had to try some sort of emergency operation on one of 'em because they couldn't breathe."

"How awful," Lars said and he let Toots talk all the way to Mercy Hospital about the ambulances and all the people that came out to watch.

When they arrived at the hospital they were told to head over to the emergency wing to see Dr. Balma who would speak to them. The receptionist was stern and would not say anything else other than speak to Dr. Balma. Lars feared for the worst but when he saw the doctor in his familiar white coat and shiny bald head he somehow felt better. Dr. Balma was the friendliest guy; his son had skied for Grayrock but now graduated. He had delivered Lars as a baby and taken his tonsils out. He met Lars and Toots in the clean warm well lit corridor of the emergency wing and spoke to them like they were adults. Lars felt funny because he was still wearing his ski boots.

"They are both all right. We had to send one of those boys to Saginaw, he's pretty bad. The other one is all right. We have them all sedated and sleeping now, otherwise I'd let you see them."

"I want to see Judy."

"Listen Lars," the doctor said, putting an arm over his shoulder and leading him away from Toots. "We have to get her ready for an operation. She's lost the baby. I understand you…" and Lars cut him off by saying quietly, "No, I wasn't. I just wanted to see her."

"Come back tomorrow morning. You men go home and pray for them. Pray for all of them."

Lars and Toots did as they were told.

On Monday in Biology class Coach Wisner was in a somber mood as was everybody else. He had written one word on the big blackboard behind him: "TRACHEOTOMY"—in big letters. Lars knew what he meant by it and what he would say about opening downstate Chuck's windpipe with a pocket knife, but he and everybody else listened intently as the coach spoke quietly. Everybody had been talking about it all morning and now they wanted to listen.

"Those girls are lucky to be alive. The police think the impact with the snowmobile was at over one hundred miles per hour. That boy's head was so badly damaged when I got there, he couldn't breathe. The snowmobiler was already dead and the others were pretty banged up but breathing. They call it "Pulling a trachea" and it's the last resort, but I had no other options. I hope some of you would have the guts to do the same for somebody someday if you had to." He expressed the last sentence with emotion in his voice and then looked out the window at snowflakes falling gently onto the jack pine trees. "Shame to hear that he died this morning. Take out your lab notes and we'll review that dissection work we did last week."

Lars got his car keys back but occasionally he would ski over to the hill for night skiing and practicing with Toots. He would stop at the outrun of the Toboggan run and look around. New snow would have covered the debris but when the snow melted in the spring it would appear. That spring Judy's dad was offered a job running a boat-making plant in Florida. She didn't come back to school and her family moved before summer and the boating season on Lake Margaret. He and Toots did a lot of water skiing that summer.

Winter Camp

The light was flat, nearly dark now under the towering white pines. We had made it to the high knoll overlooking Lake Arvon after several hours of snowshoeing into the Huron Mountains from Skanee. This was where we would set up camp and it was a good spot. The wind was picking up and blowing through the tops of the pines making a whooshing sound.

My mountaineering skis were clumsily strapped on either side of my pack frame, making it difficult to pull off my shoulders. Dougal already had his gear off, snowshoes and all. He was taking his down-filled coat off and was readjusting the bright red suspenders holding up the wool trousers on his lanky torso. He saw that I was struggling and came over and helped me. Once the pack was off I could untie my snowshoes and it was then easier to walk around the campsite. We had already tramped the snow down with our snowshoes a little and besides that the snow wasn't too deep at this time in December.

Dex and Kerry had their packs and snowshoes off and had gone to the edge of the bluff to look out over the snow-covered lake. They were planning to go ice fishing on the lake tomorrow with Dougal. I was planning to try climbing up, then skiing down Mt Sherwood, the highest point in Michigan. But first we had to set up camp before it got dark.

"How's about a little fire action, eh?!" Dougal called out to Dex and Kerry. They both turned around and nodded their heads slightly in agreement and began stomping back towards their packs. Dex had a lightweight Swedesaw in his pack and I had an axe in mine. I presumed that Dex and Kerry would go off and collect firewood and I would go cut fresh pine branches with Dougal. I started to undo the plastic catches on the pack cover and carefully pulled out the axe.

"There's some good looking boughs over there, Lars," Dougal said, pointing beyond the edge of the stand of tall pines. I turned and spotted the group of young spruce trees, each a bit bigger than an average domestic Christmas tree.

"Those will do," I said and slung the axe over my shoulder and as we walked towards the trees I said to Dougal, "I'll cut, you drag, eh?"

"Sure, Lars," was all Dougal said as we walked together and our Sorel boots sank deeper into the snow once beyond the cover of the big pines.

We all kinda knew the drill, having been winter camping several times before. It was now a bit of a tradition for the four of us to head out during the Christmas break. It was good to be together after the family action of Christmas and before the New Year blowout. And on the Monday after New Year classes at Michigan Tech would be starting up all over again. The varsity skiing team selection time trials started next week too. I had been training hard in the preseason and on the slopes at Mont Ripley and would be ready for Wednesday's slalom trial. I didn't need to think about it as I felt confident about my skiing, and it was my third year on the team. What I didn't feel confident about was Differential Equations. I'd failed another exam just before this break. I'd recover from that—I just needed to do some more studying.

What I couldn't recover from was that woman. It would do me no good to think about her either as it was over before it started, just like the rest of those women. I didn't want to think about any of it. Right now I had to concentrate on cutting pine boughs and getting the camp ready.

I went to the nearest spruce tree and began hacking at the branches about chest high. The little piles of snow still resting on the tree tumbled down on me. Soon I had needles sticking to the sleeves of my wool Mackinaw coat and my wool Pendleton trousers, but I kept on working. Dougal collected the boughs as I cut them and when he had enough to carry set off for the campsite. I moved on to another tree, having trimmed the first one neatly, and began making a stack of boughs as I cut them. The pinesap stuck to the axe blade and the boughs smelled so clean and fresh. The smell seemed like a cross between pine disinfectant and a gin and tonic. Dougal made several more trips and when he said we had enough I cut a few more branches to tidy up the last tree and dragged them back to camp.

At the camp things were getting settled already. Dougal had made two surprisingly large beds of pine boughs. They lay "side by each" about ten feet from the firepit that Kerry and Dex were constructing. Somehow those guys had found a birch windfall and dragged two large logs back to the camp. The logs were set in an L-formation bordering the firepit and would serve as our seats. They had brought back a pile of branches from the windfall and were now digging out the snow to form the firepit. I walked over to the pile of branches and began snapping them into small pieces to use as kindling.

Dougal was fishing through his pack and pulled out an oblong sack and began emptying its contents. "We ought to get these tents up, eh Lars," he said to me. I looked at the others nearly finished with shifting the snow and they nodded.

"We'll get the fire started, then do our tent," Kerry said. "You get yours up then start on supper, Lars. I'm starving."

I went over to help Dougal erect his mountain tent on top of the bed of pine boughs. It was not possible to drive tent stakes into the snow so we used guide wires. These were lengths of thin bright rope running in all directions, tied around the trunks of the big pines. I looked up as I was tying a knot and saw the treetop swaying in the wind of a darkened, threatening sky. We would have snow tonight. Dougal crawled out of the two-man tent and nodded that it was ready, perched up on top of that pile of pine branches.

Kerry and Dex had the fire going now and were turning a small pile of twigs into a roaring fire. I walked over to join them and instinctively set up my hands to the flames to warm them. They were a bit cold after doing the tent, which required removal of my wool gloves to tie knots. The light from the fire compensated for the darkness creeping in.

"What's for supper then, chef?" Dex asked, taking his gloves off and stroking the stubble on his chin. Dex was a short wiry guy like me. We'd all gone to high school together and now he and I were both studying mining engineering.

"I'll see what I can rustle up," I replied, giving the fire builders a nod of approval, then added: "The fire's cranking away."

"Those are pretty mega beds, Lars," Kerry said glancing over towards Dougal's tent perched up on the mound of pine boughs. Kerry was rummaging through his new pack and pulled out a headlamp and strapped it around his head after straightening his big bushy mop of hair. He had just come back from California for Christmas. He looked even bigger and stronger after three years of hiking and lumberjacking in the Sierras.

"Why don't youse guys get your tent up and I'll start supper," I said and went for my pack. They marched off to erect their tent in the fading light. I set my pack down beside the fire and somehow felt really comfortable with the heat and light that the fire was providing. I loved that clean pure smell of birch wood burning. And I loved winter camping.

We had split up the weight-carrying duties pretty well. Dougal and Kerry each took tents. I had the meals prepared in advance and placed them in Tupperware tubs in my pack. Dex had the frying pan and plates and such items in his pack. I pulled out one of the tubs containing the chopped up venison and another the diced potatoes. There was also the small tub with the butter, salt, and pepper. All I needed now was the frying pan. I went over to Dex's pack and opened it and began fishing through his collection of things until I found it and the spatula.

The fire had burned through the snow quickly and was now warming the forest floor. I hadn't seen dirt in what seemed like months now. Upper Peninsula winters started in October and didn't end sometimes until May and this winter was running to plan. We all made the best of it and this winter camping expedition was all part of the enjoyment. I smiled to myself and used the edge of the frying pan to scrape some hot coals away from the main blaze, which was now too hot to stand beside. The coals smoked a bit out on their own but would be fine for cooking on.

Dex had shot the buck down near the Mosquito Inn back in November. He took extra care to hang it for a few weeks in his parent's garage. Then it was carefully butchered and the meat frozen. He'd brought the slab over to my place, still frozen, a few days before when we were still planning the trip. When it had thawed we cut it up into small pieces and left it to marinate in a mixture of olive oil, garlic and spices. I had done a similar exercise with the potatoes. Nothing was going to stick to my frying pan, but I still cut off a chunk of butter and let it melt slowly in the pan just for luck and flavour.

The butter was dancing and bubbling in the pan, its sweet aroma filling the air. I bent over and pored the mixture of chopped venison and oil into the pan and put it on the heat. The pieces of meat sizzled. Then I set the potatoes into the outer circle of the pan. It was sizzling and bubbling away and would cook quickly now. With the spatula I began to turn the meat. It was already browned and looked beautiful. I called over to the others.

"Grub's nearly ready. Come 'n get it!"

"Smells great, Lars." Dex walked over with a pile of plastic plates and forks. The others followed and I began to serve up the food onto the plates, each taking a plate from Dex and getting a big portion. There was plenty to go around but we were pretty hungry. Dex held onto my plate and I dished up the last of it and then scooped up some snow into the frying pan and it hissed back at me. I set the pan and spatula down next to the fire and watched the snow in the pan begin to melt and then took the plate from Dex. We all sat down on the log and ate quietly and quickly, listening to the fire crackle and the wind rush though the tops of the trees in the darkness above.

When I had finished I made the announcement that I was thirsty. The venison was pretty salty to begin with and that, coupled with the twelve miles of snowshoeing, must have made everyone dehydrated. We all agreed to break into the half gallon of orange juice that was in the bottom of my pack. When I got up to fetch it I hadn't realized how dark and cold it was away from the fire. I had taken my Mackinaw off while cooking and, now away from the heat and rush of getting dinner ready, I felt cold and exhausted. It took my eyes a few moments to adjust to the darkness, albeit aided by the white carpet of snow all around me. It suddenly dawned on me how alone and isolated we were out here in the midst of the Hurons. I fished through my pack and grabbed the plastic jug and it felt cold and heavy, the liquid sloshing about a little as I carried it back to the others sitting around the fireside. I hadn't noticed that it was beginning to snow but the flakes were drifting down, silhouetted behind the backdrop of the fire and my friends sitting beside it.

"Looks like you'll have some fresh powder for your ski run tomorrow, Lar," Dex said as I sat down on the log and handed him the jug. He unscrewed the plastic cap and took a swig and handed it to Kerry.

"Yeah, it's starting to come down all right," I replied. "Mind you, we've had plenty already this week."

"Could be another 300-inch year," Dougal said, taking the jug from Kerry.

"At least," Kerry said before wiping his face with the back of his hand and continuing, "that OJ is pretty good. I think we'll have a real drink once our fluid level is up."

"Don't tell me," Dex said, giving Kerry a slight nudge.

Dougal handed the jug back to Kerry who handed it to Dex who gave it to me. I couldn't wait to get the liquid down my throat and I knew what Kerry was going to say but for now I was only interested in satisfying my thirst with orange juice.

"I just happen to have a little something in my coat pocket," Kerry announced and pulled out the slim glass pint bottle.

"Not that Everclear again," I stated, having had a long soothing drink of orange juice.

"The one and only."

"Should we spike the orange juice and just keep going?" Dex asked.

"No way," I stated. "We'll want to have OJ with breakfast tomorrow. That stuff is bad enough on its own."

"Are you knocking the merits of Everclear, Lars?" Kerry asked politely as he unscrewed the cap off the bottle.

"Not at all," I replied. "I just don't want it in the orange juice."

"Well, take it straight then." He handed me the bottle and added with a giggle: "And admire the excellent weight-to-alcohol ratio. You'll appreciate that as an engineer."

I grasped the bottle and took a sniff of its contents. The strong grainy aroma hit me and brought back memories of last year's winter camp and a trip made to Isle Royale during the summer. Both were accompanied by this potent liquid, which ran at something like 180 Proof.

"The strongest alcohol known to man," I said as I took a swig and felt the burning liquid race down my throat followed by the strong grainy taste in my mouth. I handed the bottle back to Kerry, muttering the only thing that could come out of my mouth: "Whew!"

"At least it's the strongest legal drink known to us men," Kerry said as he took a swig and passed it along.

"Hey Lars," Dougal said, standing up to straighten out the wool clothes clumsily covering his thin lanky frame. "You can always get a job in one of those coal mines in Eastern Kentucky when you graduate." He took the bottle from Kerry and before he had a swig stated, "And you could get into some of their moonshine." We watched his silhouette in the firelight raise the bottle to his lips and when he had finished his swig and licked his lips and shaken his body and handed the bottle to Dex said, "On second thought, that's probably not such a good idea. That stuff is lethal."

Dougal sat down eventually. The bottle was passed back and forth between us and we all took turns standing up and talking and stretching with the real intent of warming our backsides against the fire. The reality hit me like a cold wind off Lake Superior: We were all still trying to hang on. There was a world out there, waiting for us. We all wanted something, but didn't know what it was yet. For now, we were all here in the Hurons, we were all together, and it was good.

We continued drinking and talking while the fire blazed and the snow fell. When the bottle was finished I felt more tired but it was that happy sort of tired. There was nothing else to do but sit by the fire and talk, so we did that for a while and I told everyone I'd been offered a Co-op job out in Wyoming and I'd be going out there at the end of the Winter Quarter.

"What kind of mine—uranium or somethin' like that?" Dougal asked.

"No way," I said. "Not after Three Mile Island, anyhow."

"You're not scared of nuclear, are you now, Lars?" Dex asked.

"No, not at all. This is a trona mine, man. You know, that's where they get the baking soda from along with other stuff for things like glass making."

"You're full of information tonight, eh Lars," Kerry said.

"Only full of Everclear. Thanks for bringing it along." I looked up into the sky but could only see the snowflakes falling and felt them landing and melting on my face. Dougal handed me the bottle. There was only a drop left in it.

"It'll be good for you to get out west, Lars—you know, see some new places. Meet some new women," Dougal said as if that was what he wanted to be doing.

"You can always come to California, Lars," Kerry suggested. "There's plenty women there. Just your type up in the Sierras."

"You're going back?" I asked.

"For sure,"

"Count on it, dude."

"How long you gonna stay in Wyoming?" Dex asked.

"Dunno—as long as it takes, I suppose," I said slowly and poured the last of the alcohol down my throat. "I'll be back." We sat there and continued to look at the fire and listen to it crackle and felt it give off heat on what was now a snowy winter evening.

After a while I said I wanted to get some sleep and everyone agreed that we'd let the fire burn down as there was nowhere for it to go. It was easy to crawl into the tent and strip off down to my long johns once inside the sleeping bag. The bed of pine boughs was surprisingly comfortable and it didn't seem to take long to find myself warm and happy and dreaming.

When I lifted my head out of the sleeping bag it touched the sagging wall of the tent. The heavy snow in the night had accumulated onto our tent and was acting to insulate it but also threaten to bring it to collapse. I had hardly noticed when Dougal came in after me last night and when I looked over to say good morning noticed that his bag was empty. The tent was darkened from the snow lying on it but when I poked my head outside I could see it was a bright, white morning with fresh snow everywhere. My friends were snapping branches and smoke was slowly rising from the fire. They must have just restarted the fire and the birch smelt fresh burning on a beautiful morning greeting our winter camp.

"Morning, gentlemen," I said to them.

"Morning, Lars," they seemed to say in unison as the fire crackled.

"Better get your ass out of bed," Dougal said. "Nearly breakfast time."

"And you're cookin'!" Dex added.

"Wouldn't have it any other way," I replied, adding, "Bit of snow in da night der, eh?"

"You betcha. The tents are well covered. Good insulating material though, eh?" Kerry snapped more twigs and put them on the fire and I could now see orange flames rising and shimmering heat waves.

"I'll be out in a jiffy," I said, crawling back into the tent to get dressed in my outer layer of wool clothing. Even though it was an Upper Michigan winter morning it did not feel cold and I felt fresh and well rested. I slipped on the thick wool socks and then put my feet back into the Sorels. Out of the tent I went and stretched in the nice bright morning light. The fresh snow was everywhere like a new white blanket someone had left in the night. The guys had already stomped much of the snow down around the campsite and the fire had melted more of it.

The fire had also melted something else. I walked over to pick up the frying pan, which I'd left by the fire last night with it full of snow. The snow had melted and the ensuing water had evaporated and that left the spatula to melt in the heat. I reached down to pick it up and Dougal spoke.

"We wanted you to see that, Lars. Guess we forgot to lift it away from the fire."

"No biggie," I said, prying the melted plastic off the surface of the frying pan. The stem of the spatula snapped off like a birch twig.

"Definitely not thermoplastic," Dex said with a laugh.

"I guess not," I replied, holding the frying pan in one hand and a broken melted spatula in the other.

"What you gonna do now?" Kerry asked.

I looked at the big birch log we had been sitting on last night. The bark still looked fresh and white and clean like a sheet of paper.

"I'm gonna improvise," I said and finished scraping the last of the melted plastic out of the frying pan and set it down on the log. I tossed the plastic spatula onto the fire and it sizzled and released black smoke as it crumpled up and disintegrated.

I walked over to my pack leaning against the tent with a big blob of fresh snow on it. I brushed the snow off and opened the flap and began taking things out—axe, bacon in a plastic container, pancake mix in another. The bacon and the mix were frozen but that didn't matter. The orange juice was much the same.

"Dex," I ordered, "fill the frying pan up with snow and get it melting. Then stick this mix and the juice carton in it. Let's try not to let the plastic melt this time. I don't think this is thermoplastic either."

Dex did as I instructed. He grabbed a spoon and as the pancake mix and juice began to melt in the water he stirred each until they were fluids once again.

"You want me to sort this bacon out?" Dougal asked.

"Yeah. First cut a few hunks of butter off. It's in the pack. I'm gonna make a spatula." I tramped over to the log, taking the axe with me.

I carefully poised the axe along the length of the birch log lying in the snow. It would only take a single accurate swing and a nice sliver of birch would be made. My instinct was to address the log and make something like a practice swing with the axe blade set at about forty-five degrees to the log. Then slowly, accurately, almost automatically the axe came down and struck the wood and the chip of birch came flying off as though it were a wedge shot from a sand bunker. I watched the chip fly off and land in the snow and felt I had got it right the first time. Kerry was watching. He walked over to pick up the chip out of the snow.

"Nice one, Lars," he said, handing me the thin piece of wood with the white bark still attached to it. I had set the axe back beside my pack and took the chip from him. I felt its texture and smelled the fresh cleanness of the wood.

"We'll be cookin' with gas now," I said to myself and then walked back to join the others at the fire.

"Pancake sandwiches then, eh?" I announced to the others and bent down over the frying pan where the bacon was sizzling away. I used the birch chip spatula to flip the strands of bacon over, already cooked to crisp on one side. The uncooked sides began to sizzle and pop once they got hot. I picked up the orange juice and had a swig while watching the bacon cook. Then I gave the pancake mix a stir and was ready to cook.

Using the birch chip spatula again I turned the bacon over and pushed it to one edge of the frying pan. Then I spooned off a hunk of butter, using the spoon covered in pancake mix. The butter splattered and hissed in the pan and the bit of mix with it began to cook. I then spooned out good measures of pancake mix into the pan and let it cook. When enough bubbles had appeared I slid the birch chip between the hot pan and the cake, starting around the edges and gradually working my way in. When I was certain it was loose from the grip of the pan I flipped it over. I felt satisfied to see the golden brown surface of the cooked side of the pancake and smelled that reassuring aroma.

"Who's first then?" I asked the others. They were all standing there watching me and none of them spoke.

"Lars, that looks and smells outstanding," Dex finally said. "I'll be the guinea pig this time."

"Great. There's enough batter for one big pancake each. Okay if I put two pieces of bacon in the middle and wrap the pancake around it?"

"That's the ticket! At least we won't need plates."

I picked out two strips of the now crispy bacon and set them across the middle of the golden brown surface of the cake. It was swelling as the texture of bubbles on the sides expanded. Then I used the birch chip to fold the edges of the pancake over on top of the bacon. I rolled it over without anything sticking to the pan and then served it up to Dex who took it and shifted the hot pancake sandwich from hand to hand to let it cool off. He then bit into it and smiled as I started making the next one.

When we had finished our breakfast Dougal asked, "What's the plan for the rest of the day?"

"I'd still like to try out those mountaineering skis, if that's okay," I replied, sitting on the birch log now, enjoying a sunny morning sitting by the fire in the middle of nowhere. There was no wind or sound or commotion of cooking. Just a nice morning.

"We didn't bring all that ice fishing gear out here for nothing," Dex said.

"What's the hurry Dougal? You don't have a woman waiting for you back in Houghton now, do you?" Kerry kidded. We all knew that Dougal had broken up with his girlfriend a few months ago.

"Hardly," he replied. "I was just trying to figure out a plan."

"Well, that's the last of the food, unless you want to live on butter," I said.

"I was thinking maybe hiking back after mid-day then. It'd be after dark by the time we got back to the truck."

"That's alright. I've got a flashlight. Besides, if it stays clear we'll be able to cover the ground by moonlight."

"Well Lars, you've been doing all the work this morning," Dougal said. "I suggest you head off and get your skiing in. We'll clear up and break camp, pack up and all that, then get into some ice fishing action. If we catch anything we'll cook it up for lunch." He looked at me and seemed to ask the others and we all nodded in agreement.

"Use my axe for a spud," I said, getting up to put some snow in the frying pan.

I had to think about how I was going to make it up Mount Sherwood. It was my plan to use the mountaineering skis all the way there. But the fresh snow would make the going difficult. I would probably get bogged down. It probably would not hurt to take my boots and skis and snowshoes in the pack. That would at least assure me of being able to get up there. Then I would have to ski down with the snowshoes in my backpack. Everything in life was a compromise, but sometimes that was the best way to get anything done. So I decided to use the shoes and began unloading all the things out of my pack that were not needed on the mountain. I took out the borrowed pair of collapsible ski poles, deciding I would use them today even when snow shoeing. I hadn't used them when we walked in yesterday.

I set off from the camp, just giving a nod to my friends. They were cleaning up after breakfast and then getting themselves ready to go ice fishing. They nodded back to me and I set off in the opposite direction of the lake they would be fishing and began striding atop the fresh soft snow towards Mount Sherwood.

Before long I was well into the woods beyond the camp, the ground already rising. The tracks we had made in cutting the pine branches last night were completely covered over by the new snow. I took a last look down at the camp with smoke drifting gently skyward from the fire. It all looked so calm and peaceful, surrounded by the whiteness. Then I headed off through the woods in the general direction of mount Sherwood. The snowshoes felt good and I was surprisingly strong. It had been a good summer and fall doing dryland training and I was in the best shape of my life. My legs were not stiff or sore from yesterday's hike. I made steady progress and soon was passing large granite rock outcrops and scattered pine trees along with copses of birch and maple. Looking through the leafless trees provided a view towards the hills.

Before long I found myself climbing uphill at a good rate. The grade began to steepen and I could no longer go straight uphill. I would have to plan a switchback approach and it would take more time. But I was outdoors, I was feeling good, and I was enjoying it. The temperature was cold but with no wind, and it was dry and sunny. My only wish was that I had sunglasses. I pressed on, upwards always. About halfway up I began to break a sweat. By then I'd been shoeing for well over an hour and I was glad I had taken the decision to wear the shoes. The snow was deep and fluffy. It would have been difficult to ski through despite all the tales I'd heard about mountaineering skis and how good they were. All this was going to be a learning experience. I just had to be patient and make the best of it.

Another half hour of steady hiking and the pitch had become very steep and I was hot and sweaty now, the sun almost seeming to beat down through the lonely winter sky. Stopping to catch my breath and look up at the pitch I knew it was going to be a great run down. I could now look out above the tree line and off in the distance was Keweenaw Bay and the Copper Country beyond that. I always liked looking out across from the Peninsula towards these Huron Mountains when running on the Paradise Road above Chassell on hot summer afternoons, the sweat rolling off me and my mind working on setting up for turns in some race. Now I was on a pitch, sweat rolling off me on a winter morning, looking back at a Peninsula dotted with hills and trees and fields all covered in white. That all ran down to the long flat expanse of the bay, now fully frozen over and going to stay that way until April. In the distance I could see Mont Ripley, barely making out the runs and lift lines. All going well I'd be back there tomorrow and training.

But today I was going to make my way down this hill. I had to get up there first. With my mind now determined and my body rested I set off through the snow. I moved those snowshoes with a purpose now, striding up and ahead with each step, making the short switchbacks, climbing steadily until I reached the summit.

I wanted to take a moment to catch my breath again and cool off. I also wanted to take in the view to the east. So I stripped my pack off, taking care to set the skis down this time without assistance. I took my Mackinaw off and the sweater underneath. With just a long john shirt covering my torso the air felt cool and fresh. I left the ski poles behind and walked across the summit ridge and soon had the vast expanse of Lake Superior to take in. It was big, blue and beautiful, running off out to the horizon. The shore ran out and off in the distance towards Marquette. Nothing but trees and rocky hills and the vastness of the largest of the Great Lakes, and suddenly I felt so alone. I took it all in and felt grateful and then turned around and headed back to my pack to prepare for my run down Mount Sherwood.

I began my preparation by pulling everything out of the pack. Then I unstrapped the snowshoes and stood them in the snow. I sat down on the empty pack and swapped my Sorel boots for the stiffer plastic mountaineering boots I was borrowing for this run. They felt different, not as stiff as normal ski boots but much stiffer than those comfortable Sorels. I stood up to begin repacking and was surprised how far I sank into the snow without snowshoes or skis supporting me. I placed the boots and snowshoes securely into the pack and put it over my shoulders and secured it tightly to me. It felt pretty comfortable and wouldn't get in the way of my skiing. Finally I put the skis on. The skis felt strange initially, just like they had when I practiced telemarking back at Ripley. I couldn't get used to having my heel free to move around, totally relying on the toepiece and heelstrap to keep me in contact with the ski. Surprisingly, the snowshoes had helped somehow in making me more accustomed to these circumstances.

I slid over to the crest, ready now and thinking about how I was going to make my way down the steep long pitch. There were copses of pine trees in scattered spots running down the slope but otherwise it was surprisingly open. The pitch was just as I had thought when looking over at this hill from the other side of the Bay. Now I was looking towards my home out across the Keweenaw and felt good about it. I looked down at the lake past the outrun of the hill, only able to see the far side of it because of the trees. My friends would be out on the lake by now doing their ice fishing and I hoped they were successful. I was going to have a successful run down this hill and I was going to do it now.

I pushed myself through the deep snow and into the fall line and let gravity take hold. My first instinctive reaction was to lean back with both skis together and try to push my knees into a turn. But then I quickly reacted and adopted the technique of the telemark and pushed one ski in front of the other and then began the turning action and it cut through the fresh snow easily and I was away. I looked down the pitch to pick my line and thought I'd get a few turns in on this section before I reached the trees and then cut across to another clear piece of ground. I picked up speed and with that the snow began blowing up high enough to splash on my face. But I was in control now and making telemark turns, doubling poling just to make sure I had set myself up properly and glided and then turned and then made a big sweeping turn to dodge the first group of trees and continued downwards on a new pitch.

The run was longer than anything I had skied in the Midwest. I was starting to breath heavily and feel the burning in my legs and I still had a long way to go before the slope ran out and into the thicker trees at the bottom. I wasn't going to stop, having come this far. It was my chance to make a good run and I kept going, working on the rhythm of the telemark turns and keeping the action going of one ski in front of the other and then vice-versa. With the snow so soft and fluffy there was no need to set an edge and I was grateful for that and kept going down the long steep pitch.

I must have made fifty turns by the time the pitch ran out and into the trees. I let my momentum carry me and choose a line that gave me enough room and I glided on top of the snow through the woods, having to dodge trees occasionally but enjoying the glide. I started a little cross-country action as I began to slow down and was surprised at how quickly I lost my speed and sank into the fresh soft snow. I was glad I had snow shoed out and up Mount Sherwood. Then I forgot that I wanted to stop and look at my tracks. I would not be able to see them now on account of the trees. I looked behind me and saw nothing but woods running up the slope and my tracks just behind me running into the woods. I turned and headed towards the camp, keeping the skis on as it wasn't far now.

The others were all at the camp when I returned. Smoke was drifting upwards from the fire in a lazy spiral. I could see they were cooking. I t must have been a successful morning of ice fishing. Then tents were down and packed away. All that stood of the camp now were two piles of well-trampled pine boughs and the birch logs beside the fire. Dex saw me and nudged Dougal who spoke as Dex was chewing on a piece of fish.

"Hey Lars, how did the skiing go?"

"Great!" I exclaimed, pulling up to stop skiing. I bent down to start taking off the skis. Dougal came over as if to help me with my pack but I already had started removing it from my shoulders.

"Looks like youse guys did good."

"Yeah. A half a dozen walleyes. They were biting good. Didn't even have to chum the hole."

"Whadda use for bait?"

"Corn. We decided to come back and cook those babies up. Figured you'd be back by now. C'mon and have some. Kerry's doing the cooking this time."

"Smells pretty good," I said and walked over to join the others standing around the fireside. It was all so quiet and calm in the sunlight and snow and it felt like we could stay here forever. I had some fresh fish fillets cooked in butter and talked about my telemark run down Mount Sherwood. I liked listening to the fishing stories. Then it was time to go. I began hiking out of the Hurons with my friends on a sunny afternoon. We had plenty of time.

West Highland Way

When you get told to do something, you go do it. That usually makes somebody happy. Sometimes making people happy can make opportunities, like it did for me in early May in the mid-1980's. I agreed to drive a Landrover from England up to the West Coast of Scotland, towing a boat behind me. That made the boss happy. In return, it gave me the opportunity to ski in Scotland for the first time.

I had come to the United Kingdom to work a few months earlier. Before that I'd been bumming around Salt Lake, working on exploration sites. In my spare time I was trying to decide which range of mountains was best for me, and I could not decide between the Tetons, Uintas or Wastach. What I did decide was that a change would do me good, so when I was offered the job in a bar one night in Wyoming I took it. I figured it would be a good excuse to ski in Europe.

The only problem was that the mid-80's saw some pretty lean snow seasons across Europe. When I did get some time off I headed over to the Continent and came back disappointed. There was the excitement of skiing in a foreign place, but there was no substitute for good snow. There would be other years and other places, and I would be back. I was planning to stay here for a long time.

Much to my surprise, I had heard that up in Scotland good snow conditions were prevailing even past Easter. I was astounded. I made a few phone calls to check it out. Using the Directory Enquiries service from British Telecom I eventually found my way through to some Scottish Tourist Board. A pleasant lady with a pleasant Scottish accent chatted away nicely to me and wondered why an American would want to go skiing in Scotland in April but couldn't help me with much information other than the number of a place called White Corries in Glencoe. The phone number was simply 'Balla-chulish 243.' The word Ballachulish just seemed to roll off her sweet tongue. Every time I tried to repronounce it the way she did I felt like I was going to spit. I looked up the full national code for bal-a-hule-ish and made the call from my office on a Thursday morning. A rough sounding voice answered after several rings:

"Aye."

"Is that the White Corries ski area in Glencoe?"

"It is, aye."

"Are you, uh, going to be open this weekend?"

"We'll be open then, right enough. Aye, it'll all be a runnin', sun-shine or showers."

"What's the skiing like?"

"Auch, not bad, so I'm told. If the weather holds we'll get a few more weeks in."

"What's the weather like then?"

"Auch, it's blowin' a gale just now. That'll clear soon, right enough. Where you calling from lad? You sound like a Yank."

"I am. But I'm calling from a place near Bristol, down in the West Country. I heard you were still open and as I'm coming up to do some work next week thought I'd stop in."

"Well, fancy that. A Yank coming all the way up here just to ski."

"Stranger things have happened."

He chuckled. "Right enough, lad. Bring your waterproofs. Cherri-bye. Bye bye.."—and the line went dead. I set the receiver back in its cradle and decided that was it—I was going to attempt skiing in Scotland. All I had to do was get ready. I looked out my office win-dow and beyond the yard full of equipment could see thick green grass growing on the rolling hills, and yellow daffodils along the access road verge. It all seemed pretty strange indeed to be contemplating skiing at this time of year. I repeated my comment to the man on the phone a few moments earlier and tried to imitate his gruff accent, saying Ballachulish over and over again until I did spit.

By three in the afternoon I was ready to hit the road north. I had gone back to my 'digs' on the outskirts of Weston-Super-Mare to collect my things. That included my skiing gear. I had left the Landrover back in the yard as one of the fitters was giving it a service and fitting lights for the boat trailer. I had already loaded up the back of the vehicle with all the equipment I needed for a stint of exploration work on some islands in the Firth of Lorne—surveying gear, spare parts, two sets of waterproofs (the waterproofs were not so waterproof). We already had guys out on Islay getting things set up. We were to move another rig to a neighboring island called Jura. The purpose of the boat was to allow us to 'flit' between the islands, only a few hundred meters apart across the Sound of Islay.

A cement company had contracted with our little exploration company to investigate the limestone deposits on both islands. They were in a big hurry to get the information on the quality of the limestone, looking for a high calcium carbonate content. That meant drilling holes into the bedrock and recovering solid core cylinders for analysis. Why we couldn't just use one rig and do one island and then the other was beyond me. What this meant for me, as the site engineer, was that I would be doing most of the flitting between the islands. I had to survey in the drill sites, collect the cores, and log the basic information. Before now all I thought Islay was famous for was peaty flavored Whisky. I was sure Jura was much the same, although I once heard that George Orwell had written *Nineteen Eighty-Four* while living on the island. Pretty ironic that I was going there in the same year!

As I was leaving Weston on that sunny afternoon thoughts of how people and places gained notoriety dwelled on me: there was my hometown back in Michigan, famous for mining copper and playing college hockey; and then there were those islands up in Scotland, famous for their whisky and remoteness—a remoteness that inspired writers. And then there was this town of Weston-Super-Mare where, when the tide went out, the mud flats seemed to stretch out to the horizon. I heard that Weston was the home of John Cleese, the great comic of Monty Python fame. And that guy who was in the government and wrote the novels of the day, Geoffrey Archer. I supposed he would bring additional fame to Weston one day. I only had one exit to go on the M5 motorway to get off for Clevedon and wondered what notoriety I would ever achieve. Certainly not for skiing in Scotland. But that would not stop me from trying.

When I got back to the yard the boat trailer was hitched up to the back of the Landrover. One of the fitters, Trevor Fry, was standing in the back of the boat and our yard manager was standing beside the big Volvo outboard motor. I parked my car and began loading my things out. Alan McGilliciuty came over to speak to me.

"Just a little adjustment and you'll be set to go, to be sure," Alan said in his Irish accent.

"What's up?" I asked.

"That trailer is wobblin' like a bowlful of jelly. We're a takin' the motor off."

"Is that necessary?"

"If you want to go more dan tirty miles an hour, well yes lad, it's necessary."

"I'll take your word for it"

"Just take it into Currie's boatyard in Oban whenever you get there. He'll see to the fittin' out. He's expectin' ya, to be sure."

"Sounds good Alan. I'll just load up and be on my way. I'll try to make it as far as Carlisle tonight."

"Ah, Carlisle. I know it well, lad. There be a 'truck stop' as you'd say, with rooms, just off the motorway."

"Guess that's where I'll head for then."

"I used to know a fair lass up in Carlisle. That were when I wore a younger man's clothes."

"You're only as old as the woman you feel," I said with a chuckle, having heard that phrase in the pub a few nights ago. Alan laughed as well, then looked at my ski bag that I was hosting into the back of the Landrover. He held the door open just enough to keep it from touching the jockey wheel stand of the trailer and I slid the bag in, resting it on top of the middle seat. Trevor came over to look at what I was doing.

"What's in the bag then, young'un?" he asked in his West Country accent.

"It's my skis, Trev. Thought I'd have a go at it over the weekend."

"Oh, bejesus! I've seen it all now," Alan exclaimed and lifted his hands in the air and meandered his bulky frame in overalls over to the rear of the trailer. Trevor and I followed him and Trevor gave me an elbow in the ribs.

"'Ere, I 'spect the boss'd have a bit o' stuff and all lined up for a dirty weekend for ye," Trevor said quietly to me and gave me a wink. He had good hair, nice teeth and was renowned as a bird-chaser or ladies man. We all worked together to lift the motor into the back of the boat and it finally felt like I was ready. As I said my goodbyes Trevor said something like, "'Ere's to getting yer leg over," and the old Irishman just kept shaking his head and saying "Bejesus!" I started up the motor and drove out of the yard and headed for the big roundabout that was junction 20 on the M5. I looked at the ski bag resting on the edge of the seat beside me and thought how strange it seemed to be heading for Scotland to go skiing on such a sunny warm spring afternoon.

But I had to get out of England first. The miles just churned away in the slow lane of the Motorway. I had my trusty radio/cassette player in the front seat, loaded up with a fresh set of six D-cell batteries. The noise of radio stations intermixed with the odd tape from my collection kept me occupied. Traffic was not too heavy as I had beaten the rush hour in Bristol and would probably just catch the tail end of it in Birmingham. The Landrover droned on steadily and before I knew it I was past the Cotswolds and the green hills had given way to industrial scenery and I was slowing down to merge onto the M6.

The boat towed well behind the Landrover. It probably was a good idea to take the motor off and relieve the strain on the hitch and balance the load. I hardly knew it was there at times—just a slight pull when manoeuvring around slower vehicles. Soon I was out of the congestion and over the Manchester Ship Canal Bridge and heading towards the North of England as the light descended. There were fewer lorries on the road now and cars whizzed past me doing well over 100mph on the open stretches of Motorway heading into the Lake District. I passed the time trying to do mental arithmetic on estimating the speed of the faster motors by measuring distance, time and my speed. I pulled in for petrol outside of Preston and found it to be a nice spring evening. The air felt still, warm, and fresh. I took my torch out of the well in the dashboard and checked over the trailer, thinking that there were not many miles to go now before Carlisle.

On the slip ramp coming back down to the Motorway I saw two guys standing, holding a sign with "Carl" written on it. They looked about my age and had backpacks but otherwise clean and harmless. I pulled over to let them load up and take them up the road.

After we had introduced ourselves and gotten the measure of where we came from and what we were doing heading north on a Thursday night the conversation turned to movies.

"You're a yank, aye?" the wiry one called Gregor asked in such a thick Scots accent that I could barely understand him.

"That's right," I replied.

"So have ye seen the movie *Local Hero* yet aye?"

"Can't say that I have. I've heard about it though."

"Aye, it's this yank that comes over ta here an' he canna get away."

"An' he falls in with the locals and gets on, aye," the other skinny fellow with red hair added.

"This lad here is a bit like that oilman, eh Hamish?"

"He is, right enough."

"Did you know they filmed part of it right up on the west coast?"

"No, I didn't," I replied, assuming that anything about the oil business in Scotland would have had to be done in Aberdeen over in the east.

"They did some scenes up by Araisaig, the ones on the beach."

"Aye, but the village was over on the east."

"Funny what they do in movies, isn't it?" I injected in their argument.

"Anyhow, mate, you're our local hero for giving us a lift."

"Aye, we came down from Mallaig lookin' for work."

"Mallaig," I said and nodded. "Where's that?"

"It's up there on the west coast, mate, just up the road from Araisaig."

"If you ken call that a road," the other was quick to comment.

"Aye, it's a bit like going to the end of the earth to get to Mallaig, right enough."

"Sounds like where I come from," I commented.

"Where's that?" they both seemed to ask at the same time.

"The Upper Peninsula of Michigan. They say it's not the end of the earth, but you can see it from there."

We all laughed together and talked about our hometowns and work and what we wanted to do in life and before I knew it I was pulling off the Motorway for Carlisle. Then one of them asked what was in the canvas bag suspended across the seats.

"My skis," I replied, not afraid to tell them.

"Auch! He's a skier, Hamish!"

"Now isn't that a wee surprise," Hamish replied. "Surely you're not going skiing?"

"Yes, I am. Thought I'd check out that place in Glencoe."

"Aye. Now that's a small world. We both used to work there. Lift operators."

"Did you ski?" I asked.

"Auch aye. Miss it just now, having to go out and earn a wage."

"I know the feeling," I replied, thinking about how little I'd been skiing in the past year.

"Aye, there's still snow there, right enough. I was speaking to my Gran a few weeks ago. She runs a guesthouse in the village. I used to stay there when workin'."

"Our kit is still there," Gregor added.

"What's the name of the place? I'll need somewhere to stay. I was planning to stay overnight anyhow."

"Aye, Mrs MacIntrye's. Right in the village. That's me Gran, right enough."

I held out my hand for him to shake as we rolled off the motorway and followed the signs.

"Good to meet some fellow skiers."

I offered my hand to Gregor as well. They were both smiling and we all felt happy to have something in common.

"Guess we'll be getting off here."

"Well, good luck trying to find work."

"Thanks, mate. Good of you to give us a lift, right enough."

The lads said they were going to hitch into town and I said not to bother, as I would be glad to run them in and then come back out to the lorry park for the night. They offered to buy me a pint for my trouble and I reluctantly refused, saying it would be difficult to park the trailer; besides, I had a feeling that one pint would lead to another with these guys—not a bad thing but I had a mission to complete.

I found the lorry park back by the Motorway and pulled up in front of what looked like a reception. The place looked like it was of temporary construction, like the portacabins we used as offices. I walked inside and found myself in a makeshift bar of sorts. The place was full of lorry drivers sitting at small round rickety tables with pints of beer in front of them and ashtrays full of cigarette ends and more butts on the floor. The room was a haze of smoke. A lone woman stood behind the bar with several of the drivers leaning over it, clutching their pints and chatting to her. She was in her forties, overweight, smoking a cigarette and obviously drunk. Once I caught her attention I asked if there were any rooms available. She asked me what I wanted to drink and then took a pile of keys out from underneath the bar and told me to take my pick. I told her I didn't want anything to drink, just wanted a room that I could park the Landrover and trailer outside of. She fumbled through the keys and slid one of them out at me and said it was around the back. I was tired and just wanted to get out of that bar and get some sleep. She told me it was twenty quid and I had to pay now which I did gladly, leaving a fresh note on the bar before turning to leave the lorry drivers staring and laughing at me.

The next morning I was up early and had a shower and felt pretty hungry. I hadn't had much to eat since lunchtime yesterday. There was certain to be one of those nice cafes along the roadside, famous for their big breakfasts. I was feeling good despite my hunger and looked forward to being on the road. I flicked on the television to catch the morning news but all I found was some bearded guy lecturing about quadratic equations and another bearded guy chatting about being back home again. I listened for a minute to his friendly voice saying how good it was to be back home again while he sat in a studio, acoustic guitar perched on his lap, pretty English girl with the peroxide blonde hair opposite him smiling slyly. He broke out into a song about being back and it sounded pleasant enough and I felt good about being away from home but wondered when I would be longing to go home too. No time to be sentimental, I said to myself, and packed my bag and headed out the door into a steel-gray dawn.

The whine of the Landrover and the noise of the cassette player kept me company while the miles rolled away and I towed that boat and trailer towards Scotland. I pulled into a transport café just over the border beyond Gretna Green before Lockerbie to have that breakfast I was dreaming about—two eggs; bacon; sausage; baked beans; and a slice of that dark sausage called black pudding. I washed it down with a couple of cups of tea (I had already given up on the bitter tasting coffee) and paid for with a meager two pounds in cash. I was feeling good about being out on my own and doing this transport job. Then I would get a chance to do that skiing. I couldn't wait and had this sensation of lonely freedom and happiness that comes with doing something and having something to look forward to.

Over the crest of a hill on a concrete dual carriageway called the M74 I caught sight of Glasgow in the distance—high rise buildings on hillsides and urban sprawl running down to the Clyde Estuary with the blue waters of the Firth to the left beyond it. I was somehow reminded of Marquette coming into view after a long drive through Upper Michigan, only a reverse image and more urbanization making it different. At that time in the morning the rush hour hadn't started yet and I cruised steadily right through the city center on a wide cross-town Motorway and out again, crossing the Clyde twice and being alongside Loch Lomond before I knew it. That's when it started to drizzle.

I had to flick on the windscreen wipers and listen to their slow methodical action of clearing the water drops away. It was the sort of drizzle intermittent wipers would normally deal with. The only problem was that was not a feature on this vehicle. So before long I became a little annoyed at having to turn them on and off repeatedly, reaching up above me on the top of the windscreen for the switches while negotiating the twists and turns in the road. The combination of a call of nature and my frustration made me pull into a lay-by alongside the Loch and I went up into the woods.

On my return down to the loch side I found another car had pulled in behind the trailer. An older man had stepped out of his vehicle and was looking the boat over. We chatted about the drizzly weather and he wanted to know if the boat was for fishing and I told him it wasn't and that I was just delivering the boat to Oban. He joked that it was a long way to come from America just to deliver a boat. He said he was going fishing himself. He told me he thought the boat would be good for mackerel fishing. There was good mackerel fishing off Oban in August, he said while assembling his fishing pole. I wished him luck along the shores of Loch Lomond early on that quiet lazy morning with the drizzle drifting down and then watched him wander down to the water's edge. I somehow felt like I didn't have anything better to do for a while so I went back to the Landrover and found my camera among my things. I used the battered up Yashica to take a few photos of that quiet peaceful morning. I felt contented and watched the old man casting his line out into the flat calm water. When I looked up at those round-topped mountains with traces of snow on the summits shrouded in wisps of cloud I felt like I'd arrived and had all the time in the world.

By the time I reached Oban the drizzle had turned into a heavy rain. The tide was in and filled the half-moon shaped harbor. The rainfall was pockmarking an otherwise flat sheet of water. I drove through the quiet town center and past the railway station and ferry terminal and then along the coast below rocky bluffs until I reached the boatyard next to the Northern Lighthouse Board pier. I pulled in with a sense of relief that I'd made it and stopped the engine. An old man wearing a flat cap came towards me, buttoning an old tattered wax jacket against the rain. I rolled the window down and he spoke in a soft Highland voice.

"Aye. You're here. Where's the motor?"

"In the stern. We had to take it off as the trailer was towing so badly."

"Did you disconnect the controls?"

"No. It's still all hooked up."

"Aye," he said and shook his head, then looked back towards the building he had come out of. "Think you can back it into yon shed, lad?"

"I'll try," I said and watched him in the wing mirror amble back to the weatherworn building and push on a sliding door, which opened easily for him. I looked across to the offside mirror and saw him standing there by the door, now open, slowly waving his hand but giving a glare that told me to get on with it.

"Get this right the first time," I said out loud and opened my door to look back and check the position of the trailer and then glanced at the orientation of the front wheel of the land rover. I decided to pull forward first and straighten up, just the way I'd do it with a hay wagon at my Grandpa's farm every summer. I was reminded that it wasn't summer by the cold rain running down my neck as I looked back again and then checked the offside mirror as I put the vehicle in reverse, revved the engine and guided it into the shed, taking it all the way to the back where it was dark until the old man's hand signals told me to stop. The Landrover was three-quarters under cover so I didn't have to reach for my coat and just climbed out.

The first thing I noticed in the shed was the smell of freshly cut wood. There was a long workbench running along the wall on my side. In the dim light I saw all manner of tools hanging on the wall. This was a proper boat builder's place; it just had that feeling of the wood and the sea. And here I was with a fiberglass-hulled boat and a big outboard engine. I could see the old man come around with a short wooden ladder and prop it squarely against the hull and climb up to have a look in the boat. I walked over so I could hear what he had to say.

"Aye, those cables should be kept to a one meter radius. They might be damaged."

"Oh," I said, feeling a twinge of worry come over me. I remembered the heap of cables and fuel lines all still connected to the engine lying in the back of the boat. I peered over to look myself but it all looked relatively neat the way we had stowed the engine.

"But its' no bother, lad. We'll fit it all up and check her over, have her ready for Monday morning. Forecast's good for then."

"What's it like for the weekend?"

"A wee bit unsettled, just like today. High pressure moving in late Saturday, maybe."

"That sounds encouraging. Have you been told about the extra fuel tanks?"

"Aye. They're over in the corner. Your Canadian cousin has already been round to check up. He'll be glad to see you made it, lad."

"Good job," I said, smiling at the old man. "Thanks for all your help. I take it you're Mr Currie."

"Aye, that's correct. I take it you'll be wanting to check in with Paul just now. I'll tell you how to find his digs, seeing as how I organized it for him in the first place."

"Sounds like you've been giving us lots of help."

"No bother. Glad to see you lads going off to work. Maybe some of the lassies in the town will get a chance to draw breath now." We both laughed together and I told him I wasn't planning to spend much time in Oban this weekend as I wanted to go skiing and he looked at me as though I was planning to go to the moon while we unhitched the trailer.

I drove back to the other side of the small bay fronting the town and the rain kept falling. Mr. Currie's directions were pretty easy and I laughed to myself about his comments about the young women here in Oban. I couldn't wait to see what they were like, but that would have to wait for another weekend. I still wanted to ski tomorrow, despite the steady rain reminding me of its presence with its drumming on the body of the Landrover. I had turned the engine off and otherwise it was a quiet, damp Friday morning outside what I presumed was my boss Paul's digs in Oban.

I knocked on the door of the small stone cottage up a side street from the waterfront. There was no reply after waiting a while with the rain falling on me. I could tell it was his place from looking in the door window to see the familiar waterproofs hanging on a peg in the small entrance hall and the stack of boxes nearly blocking up the place. I figured they were the last of the supplies to go out to site on the boat on Monday. Getting somewhat tired of the rain I decided to try the doorknob. It was open so I walked in, taking my coat off and hanging it over his. The place was quiet but cluttered, dirty dishes and empty wine bottles on a small table in a lounge sparsely furnished with worn couches and a small television and radio cassette like mine in a corner. A narrow ladder ran steeply up from that corner into what I presumed was a loft and sleeping space. I heard a bit of rumbling up there and called out.

"Anybody home?" Inaudible whispering, then giggling was the initial response—but then came that familiar voice.

"That you eh, Lars? I'll be down in a minute. Make yerself at home. Coffee's in the kitchen, eh."

I didn't reply, just smiled and nodded to myself and went over to the kitchen at the back of the other side of the small house. A partition wall partly separated the kitchen/dining area from the lounge. I found the toilet and made use of it while the kettle boiled. I made instant coffee for both of us and thought it would be good to take out a third cup but didn't fill it. There was long-life milk in the refrigerator and I put a dash into Paul's cup. I took my coffee black and began sipping it. It tasted good after a long drive. I heard footsteps up in the loft and then the sound of someone descending the ladder. Paul appeared around the corner, his dark hair in a mess, large hands scratching an unshaven face. He tucked the tails of a partly buttoned flannel shirt into baggy sweatpants and offered me his hand. I took it and while exchanging a firm handshake handed him the coffee with the other.

"Glad you made it, Lars. Been to the boatyard yet?"

"Just left there. I met your Mr. Currie"

"He's some character, eh?"

"Yeah. Does she take coffee, or tea?"

"Oh, tea. But I'll get it. She's pretty fussy."

"Local girl?"

"Not exactly. Comes from Liverpool. Been here a while though. Works in one of the hotels."

I watched him make the tea, going through the motions of putting a teabag into a small teapot followed by boiled water from the kettle. Next was a drop of milk into the mug, then a stir of the pot. He slowly poured the light brown steaming fluid into the mug and added a spoonful of sugar.

"Won't be a minute, eh. Make yourself comfortable." He walked back for the ladder carrying the mug. I sat down at the kitchen table and thought about some of the crazy drunken adventures I'd experienced with Paul. Sometimes we would end up in trouble with women and I felt I scored more often than he, and sometimes felt sorry about that. It appeared there was nothing to feel sorry about now. He came back down quickly, full of enthusiasm.

"So, here we are, eh Lars! Another town, another site." He picked up his mug from the table, hoisting it as though it were a toast.

"And another woman," I said in reply, glancing up at the ceiling.

"She wants you to meet some of her friends. Thought we'd go out and have a few beers tonight."

"I kinda figured we'd be doing that. All divorcees I suspect, eh?"

"A few. Also a few closet deviants, so I'm told."

"It's what makes the world go round. I'd rather not do too much power drinking though."

"You on the wagon or somethin'?"

"No, I just wanted to go skiing tomorrow."

"Lars, it's May, for Pete's sake!"

"Coulda fooled me," I said glancing out the window at the rain hammering down. "I hear they still have snow."

"Well, they still have women in Oban and you're gonna meet them tonight."

"Whatever you say, boss. I take it I can stay here tonight? Thought I'd stay up in Glencoe tomorrow then get back here for Sunday night."

"Sounds like you've got it all planned out."

"How is everything shaping up on the sites?"

"Better now that you're here. But we're gonna need some help. Freddie's over on Islay right now and I've got Joe to look after the new rig on Jura. You're going to jump between the two sites to stay on top of the cores and the surveying. I've found one laborer for Isaly but can't leave Joe on his own."

"What happened to Steve and Ted?"

"They've been sent to a site in the Midlands. Some site investigation, soils and clays."

"What does that leave you to do then boss?"

"Once I get this set up?" He leaned back in his chair and sipped his coffee and thought for a moment, then replied: "I've got some 'accommodating' to do."

We were both laughing like we usually did until we heard sounds coming down the ladder. She came around the corner and I could tell she was flustered. Her long black hair was in a mess and she was tucking a white blouse into tight black trousers. The thing I noted first was her long pointed nose and intense green eyes. Then she spoke as though in a hurry.

"I'm late. I'm late. And I haven't even had me toast. I need me toast!"

"I'll see to that, Penny," Paul said standing up to help. "By the way, this is Lars."

I stood up as well and offered my hand to her. She had a brush in her other hand and after shaking mine turned to sort her hair out, using a mirror on the wall. I just stood there looking her over, not saying a thing for a few moments to give us a chance to admire each other. When she had enough of using the mirror to check me out while pretending to concentrate on her hair Penny faced me again.

"You're shorter than I thought. Oh, but cuter." She smiled and looked me over. "Nice bottom, too. You'll do just fine. Me mates are just dying to meet you. I need a wee."

She rushed into the toilet and I turned to Paul and shrugged my shoulders.

"I hardly understood a word she said."

"She's what they call a scouse. You'll get used to the accent."

"Seems pretty nice, Paul. You've done well."

"There's more where she came from," he said as the toast popped out and he began to spread butter on it.

❧   ❧   ❧

I found myself running in the rain along the waterfront Esplanade in Oban the next morning. It was still early enough. I was determined to get on the road despite my groggy head and the rain lashing down. My cowboy boots were soaked through and my hair was wet. I finally saw a taxi cruising past and I thought about flagging it down but I was nearly back at Paul's place now. I stopped running and walked a while in the rain, running my hand through my soaking wet hair and thinking how crazy I was last night. The air had that springtime feeling to it but off in the distance I could see snow still lying on the summits to the West. I presumed those were peaks on the Isle of Mull and the Morvern Peninsula. I looked out to sea towards Jura and wondered what the terrain would be like out there. I figured I'd be finding out soon enough. I kept walking in the rain, gradually feeling better.

The door was open so I just walked into the cottage. It had that early morning air of desertion to it, but I figured Paul and Penny were back now and sleeping it off. I tried to be as quiet as I could after removing my wet things. I switched the kettle on. I had time for a shave and a shower and felt pretty dirty but not ashamed. It would all be soon forgotten and chalked up to yet another night in some town near some site. There was nothing right now that made me want to change my life so I was going to make the best of it.

When I came out of the shower Paul was standing in the kitchen, leaning against the counter with his arms folded waiting for the kettle to boil. I had my toilet bag in my hand and a towel wrapped around my waist. Paul was back in his flannel shirt and sweats. We both looked at each other and shook our heads. He spoke first.

"Pretty wild, eh?"

"There's been worse."

"All that beer in the Claredon did my head in."

"Yeah. Maybe we were a little too quick on the stuff after that sauna." We had been to the Oban Sports Center yesterday afternoon before the drinking started. "You're probably right. It didn't affect your performance or powers now, did it?"

"No, Penny's pretty good at getting things outta me, if you know what I mean."

"She looks the demanding type."

"What about you, 'eh?" he asked, slyly raising an eyebrow in my direction.

I paused and then stared at him as though about to give him one of those 'a gentleman-never-tells' responses. He knew me too well. "Ever done duty on a 'Heavy Cruiser'?" I said, using what I remembered of her accent and we both laughed so hard we barely heard the kettle boiling.

"I'm sure she looked after you well, Lars. She seemed to want you real bad. Planning to see her again?"

"I dunno," I announced with an air of finality, taking the loaf of Mighty White bread out of the small refrigerator to begin making myself some breakfast. Paul took the cue that it was no longer his business and made the hot drinks and headed for the ladder. I walked after him.

"I'll see you Sunday night," I said quietly.

"No need to be quiet. She's awake. Awaiting a full report on your activities."

"Tell her I'm still alive. All bodily functions intact and operating normally."

Before long I was driving up the hill out of Oban. The rain had stopped and cloud seemed to be lifting. It would take well over an hour to drive along this coast and up the pass to the ski area. I had plenty of time and was going to enjoy the drive. That long hot shower had washed all her smells off me and it was all behind me now and I was looking forward to my skiing. I took my time and looked at the scenery, stunning to the eye even on a dim day like this one. I slowly meandered over the one-lane Connel Bridge with the rapids they call the Falls of Lora beneath me. From that high spot I could see out to Mull and the broad watery expanse of the Firth of Lorne.

A little later I was alongside Loch Crerran. There were rocky outcrops and trees running up the slopes of the mountains. It was all much closer now, like I had gone into the interior. I was still following the coastline along a narrow twisting road with my head still hurting and body aching but wanting to go skiing.

After I passed Appin and the Castle Stalker another Loch was on my left for viewing as I cruised at good speed. The road was a new one, replacing the bits of single track and twisting sections behind me. I could look out at the massive range of Mountains on the other side of Loch Linnhe. A mixture of peat, grass and rock ran up to a plateau and then snow–covered summits in the distance. Aside from the mountains and the loch there was little else. Then something reminded me that there were other inhabitants in this huge vacant land: A large red deer with a well-developed set of antlers meandered out in front of me onto the road. I rammed the brakes on and the Landrover swerved from side to side. The stag looked at me and almost gracefully bounded off the road, cleared a fence with ease and kept going into the woods. I was at a full stop, waiting for my heart to stop racing while I watched the majestic creature continue on his way as though nothing had happened. I had a whiff of the rubber I'd left on the road and put the vehicle into gear and drove off for Balla-chulish, considering myself pretty lucky.

There was only the long steady drive up the pass ahead of me. Although the climbing and whining of the engine reminded me of making my way to other ski areas, there was something totally differ-ent about this trip. It was either the remoteness or the ruggedness or the oldness of it all. I couldn't figure out which, but I was soon on the single-track road heading for a nearly empty car park with a small shed as a lodge and a chairlift running up into the clouds. I made my preparations and gathered my gear. Wearing ski boots for the first time in months felt clumsy. There was a man at the lift station who sold me a strange looking ticket for eight pounds.

"What's the deal on the ticket?" I asked, examining what looked more like a luggage tag with a line of crosshatches along its border.

"Aye, every time you use the lifts they'll punch yer card there." The man pointed to the card while adjusting his Sherlock Holmes-type cap. I recognized his voice as the one from my telephone call. I won-dered what else he did.

"What happens when I run out of punches?"

"Auch, no bother on a day like today. You'll probably have some left over which you can use another day. It's supposedta be fine tomorrow."

I counted ten marks on either side of the card. Twenty runs. I'd do that in a morning, or so I thought.

"Guess I'll be heading up then. Do you get to do the first punch?"

"Auch noo. That's already taken for. Leave your skis off lad. You'll be walking once you get off this lift."

"I thought you said there was plenty of snow."

"Auch aye. But you have to make your way to it. Say, you're the Yank who phoned. You made it."

"I guess so."

"Welcome to Scotland, right enough. Wish we had a wee bit better weather for you today. I won't keep you now." He stuck out a thick hand and I gave it a shake and a smile and he walked out of the hut to help me board an antiquated one-man chairlift.

So up I went, skis and poles perched on the edge of the rusty steel frame of the chair. My feet dangled below me and I looked down at the heather and gorse and grass as the lift carried me upwards. Soon I was looking down at streams of white water rushing down the mountainside, scoured through the peat and running over a hard surface of granite. The water roared and whooshed over a waterfall and it all seemed spectacular but so unlike being in a winter setting. It was not raining so I had elected not to don the waterproofs and felt warm enough in a pair of ski trousers and a sweater.

I was sweating after the next half hour after getting off the first chairlift. Ahead of me was something of a path that went off into the mist and low cloud. It all seemed so eerie and quiet as I set off, skis over my shoulder and boots tramping though saturated ground of muddy peat and heather trodden over by others before me. I was on a sort of plateau with a gentle grade running in the direction of what I hoped would be the snow line. I looked at this morning's hike as a way to loosen up my muscles before a day of skiing and kept hoping that this was just an inversion or low cloud and soon I'd be skiing in bright sunshine and on nice soft spring snow.

My hopes were never realized that day. The mud and water ended with the beginning of the snow at a shed made of corrugated iron. I presumed this was the lodge. I could see other skiers milling around now and hear the sound of generators running to power the lifts. I still could not see anything that resembled a lift or a run but put my skis on anyhow and made my way across corn snow in the direction of the noise.

I soon discovered what the difference was in this place. The difference was the dampness. The cloud level was sitting even with the snow level on this dark mountainside and I'd say the cloud was winning. The air felt pregnant with moisture.

It startled with a drizzle while I was riding up a T-bar, my first chance to feel snow running beneath my skis in months. I didn't mind at first. I'd skied in rain before. But when I tried to ski down on unfamiliar terrain in a cloud it became more of a challenge. The mist would stick to the lenses of my goggles. With the goggles off visibility was not much better. All I could do was try to make my way down, keeping within hearing distance of the lifts as a guide. Sometimes I could not tell whether I was skiing downhill or uphill. I had no idea what the terrain or the scenery looked like. I was just surrounded by the misty whiteness and couldn't do anything about it. Then the mist turned to rain.

So I began to get wet, really wet. The rain was not just a sudden shower. It was a steady, unceasing, unrelenting downpour. First my gloves started to leak through and became all soggy. Then my ski pants, starting at the front but then extending around to the bottom and up the crotch. Then right through my coat and onto shoulders and arms and chest and right to the armpits. I was wet from that rain and now beginning to feel a little cold. Up until the rain I had been warm and really quite dry. Now the only part of me that was dry were my feet, encased in the impregnable plastic ski boots. One more trip up to the summit and I would make my way off that mountain.

One benefit that the rain gave was to drive some of the mist away and improve the visibility. I could now make out where I was going. I found that the pitches were really pretty narrow and lined with rock outcrops. I was really skiing in gullies that the snow had either fallen or been blown into. Some of the gullies did not quite follow the fall line. So one had to make a few turns, then traverse across to the edge of the rocks, make a few more turns, and traverse again. I could now make out the bare rugged mountains, devoid of trees and in a state of near darkness at midday from the heavy thick black clouds heavy with moisture. I made my way back down to the shed where the snow line gave out, took my skis off and began that trek across the plateau to the car park chairlift.

For the first time that morning a lift attendant came out of the comfort of his hut to check my ticket. It was windy now on that station and I couldn't make out what he was saying as he punched my card. That was the only one I'd had that morning. I stuffed the ticket back into my jacket pocket carefully as it was also wet but had not started to disintegrate yet. Down I went to the car park and the relative warmth of the Landrover. I was fairly warm after my fast annoyed hike across the plateau, my sweat mixing with the soggy clothes.

The first thing to do was get out of the wet gear. I stripped down until I was naked in the back of the Landrover. Fortunately I had brought my sweats along with the clean clothes I'd worn on the drive up earlier that morning. All my other things, aside from a toilet bag, towel, and site gear, were back at Paul's cottage. It was a nice feeling to put dry clothes on again, even if it was just a pair of old baggy sweats. I dried my wet mop of hair with the towel and set it on the seat back. Then I tried to hang the other ski clothes so that they might dry out a little. I even took the lift pass out and set it on the dashboard to dry. Tomorrow would be another day.

I sat down in the back of the Landrover and thought for a while what I should do. For once I felt pretty deflated. Here I was, sitting in the quiet of a car park at the top of a desolate lonely mountain pass in Scotland. I had been defeated by a morning's rain. It would have been all too easy just to pack everything up, head down the pass and find a place to stay. An afternoon beside an open fire with a newspaper appealed right now. But then I would get bored with that and meander down to a bar and taste the beer and check out the talent. I had done nothing to deserve those pleasures. It was not what I came here for. I reached down to the floor and pulled out the bulky bright orange waterproofs. They were still covered in oil and grease from the last site I'd been on down in Devon. They would do nicely here. I also had a pair of rubber gloves and my tattered baseball cap, the Michigan Tech logo partly torn away. It didn't feel like I was going back out to ski but out I went.

I strolled back up to the lift station. The old man came out to greet me again. He looked me over in the heavy gear I had donned.

"Aye, looks like you're goin' fishin', lad."

"Feels that way. Does it always rain like this here?"

"Sometimes it's worse. Got your ticket to punch?"

"On darn. I left it in the Landrover to dry out."

"No bother. You deserve a few free ones on a day like today. You're keen, right enough."

"More like crazy," I replied and rode back up that lift into clouds swirling around the mountain and rain lashing down. Nothing seemed to bother me now.

As I drove back down the pass later that afternoon I felt better. My hangover was gone; time having been the great equalizer. My legs felt good from the afternoon's skiing. That was probably because I had not skied very hard. It was awkward skiing with all the waterproof gear on. I still managed to get wet in places. But not that total wetness I'd experienced in the morning. The visibility had improved and I was glad I had gone out for the rest of the day. I must have stood out like a sore thumb in those bright waterproofs, but I didn't care. I had done my skiing and now was driving. As I came around the bend approaching Glencoe village I could look out at the water of Loch Leven now glimmering in the afternoon sunlight. Further to the west was the Ballachulish Bridge spanning the narrows with mountains running up either side from the shores. And in the distance beyond more shimmering flat calm water were distant mountains, jagged and snow-capped. It was all so peaceful, as though it were spread out for me to view and forever leave as a snapshot in my mind after the dark foggy wildness up on the mountain.

I turned off the main A82 road just past the petrol station and headed up the village street. It was just how the two lads I'd picked up hitchhiking had described it—a few houses all of different makes and shapes lining the street. Then a church made of huge blocks of granite. Small shops on either side of the road. And just before a humpback bridge over the rain swollen white water of the river Coe, a turning to the right. I followed that road along the river for a short distance until I saw the small sign for Mrs MacIntrye's guesthouse. There was a narrow drive up beside the house, then a wide parking area behind it. I parked the Landrover and stepped out to take in the view of mountains all around me, the shape of the Pap of Glencoe seeming like it was directly above where I stood. I walked up to the door to see if any rooms were available.

The welcome was a good one. Mrs MacIntyre pleasantly put me in a small clean room in her house. No other guests had arrived yet but she said others were coming later and I was free to use the bath at the end of the hallway. I told her about her grandchildren and picking them up hitchhiking in the north of England; all she said to that was "Auch, those boys," adding that dinner would be at seven if I wanted any.

I fell into a nice hot bath, the water peaty brown in color. Soon all my bad thoughts of a wet day on the mountain in poor visibility were out of my head, replaced by ones of it being a better day tomorrow. I could hear the sounds of other guests arriving and chatting to the host in their various accents.

Over dinner we made our greetings and made conversation over what each other did for a living. I talked for too long with a well-educated Welsh couple about the coal mining industry and what this Ian MacGregor guy was going to do with it. We developed a long and balanced discussion about the relative lack of mobility in the British workforce. Mrs MacIntryre brought us all back to earth while clearing the plates and cutlery away. She said he'd do well with it because it needed shaking up and besides he belonged to Kinlochleven, which was clearly a good thing to her. I politely agreed but the Welsh were politely skeptical.

While we were finishing our sherry trifle and moving on to other subjects like nuclear non-proliferation, the doorbell rang. Mrs MacIntyre went to answer it and probably disappoint some weary travelers. But we soon heard the sound of young male voices, somewhat familiar to me. I heard footsteps and commotion in the corridor in the private part of the house and then Mrs MacIntyre came waddling back in with a big smile on her face.

"Sorry about that. Some of my grandchildren just arrived. I believe you've met them before, young man." She looked in my direction and they entered the room behind her.

"It's him, right enough," the fellow called Hamish said to the other. I stood up to shake their hands and greet them again.

"What happened to Carlisle?" I asked.

"There weren't any jobs goin' that were for us," he replied.

"We wanted some outdoor work with the summer a comin'," said the one named Gregor.

"So you're back here now," I said.

"Aye, we hitched up today. Thought we'd head back towards Mallaig next week. Didya get out skiing?"

"I guess you'd call it that."

"Aye, a wee bit wet then."

"I only got soaked through once."

The Welsh couple laughed at that as they had been out hill walking in the rain. They made a hello and good-bye to the boys and headed back to their room without saying goodnight to me. We all just stood there for a moment in the small dining room looking at each other.

"It can get wet up there, right enough," Hamish said to continue the conversation.

"Looks like it'll be better tomorrow. Take it you'll be heading back up again," Gregor added with a hint of enthusiasm.

"I didn't come this far not to."

Mrs MacIntyre butted in politely. "Aye, why don't I get you boys some tea? You must be starving."

"Right enough, Gran," Hamish said and turned to me and nodded his head with the answer he expected before asking the question. "And afterwards we have to get you that pint we promised in Carlisle."

"I could use a beer after a day like today," I said with a smile and knew I would get along fine with these guys in the pub.

❁   ❁   ❁

We had all decided to go skiing together during our evening's drinking session in the bar tied to the Glencoe Hotel. It was an inevitable decision, the type you know you are going to make because it's what you want to do. I explained I'd had a pretty heavy night (in more ways than one) the night before in Oban and didn't really need another. But these two guys kept introducing me to the other locals at the bar and each one of them wanted to buy me a drink and ask me about America, then tell me some story, either about Yanks here in the war or Canadians on the hydro or smelter plants. We got along well and soon I had to stumble back with them to the guesthouse, grateful that it was a short walk to the other side of the village, made even shorter by cutting through the police station's front garden.

After breakfast we loaded up the Landrover. It didn't take long to head back up the pass and park at the foot of the slope. It was a calm, clear, morning, the only sound being the water rushing past in a stream carrying snowmelt and yesterday's rain down the mountain. The sun was up and flooding bright light onto the face of what my Scottish friends called "The Buckle"—a steep imposing menace of a mountain rising to a rocky pinnacle. Snow and ice was packed into the rocky gullies and ravines. The surrounding hills looked tamer with their rounded tops and surfaces of brown-green grass and heather, occasional rock outcrops jutting out, patches of snow running along summit ridges.

It seemed more like a day to be out mountain climbing, or hill walking as these guys called it. They had been describing all of the peaks and ridges and walks as we drove up the pass, imparting their local knowledge of the rough sounding Gaelic names. But we were going skiing and had our gear on. I had my ticket from yesterday with me and showed it to the lift attendant, the same one as yesterday. He punched a hole in one of the markings and smiled at me, then looked at the others and shook his head.

"How did you run into these nutters?"

"I picked them up hitch-hiking the other day. They came up last night."

"Aye, mind how you go with them, lad. They're nutters. Nutters!" He raised his eyes to the heavens, a clear blue sky, as we walked towards the chairlift. Then he looked me over.

"I dina think you'll be needin the waterproofs today, lad!"

"Aye, they can go back on the fishin' boat," Hamish responded. "It's gonna be a bonny day up there,"

"Just you lads take it easy with our American friend here."

"Auch aye, Donnie, We'll l start out on the Flypaper and work it from there."

"Bleeding nutters, the pair of them," he said, grabbing the one-man chair to slow it down and let me have a seat and a ride up the mountain and everything seemed so much brighter and cleaner.

Our walk across the plateau didn't seem so lonely and desolate this time. Instead, it was almost triumphant, heading out across the moorland. The air was so fresh and clear, only slightly chilling as it filled my lungs. The ground underfoot was like walking on a sponge, water squishing out with each step onto the heather and peat. All around were the summits of mountains, resplendent in their morning glory. I chatted with the lads and they pointed out the landmarks and told stories of railways and road cuts and the remote desolation of these Highlands. Soon we were at the snow line and the base lodge and were putting our skis on for a day on the mountain.

What a difference a day made. Yesterday I was up in this fog, barley able to see my hand in front of my face, soaking wet, alone, disoriented. Today I was up in the sunshine, taking in the views, feeling the still-hard snow beneath my skis, breathing in the air, and almost tasting it. Yesterday I skied by sense. Today I would let my senses enjoy themselves. And I was with these lads that I had met purely by chance and they were going to show me around their mountain. I was looking forward to it on a fine April morning in Scotland.

We started out by riding the draglifts to the summit. The snow was still hard up there, having frozen overnight. But the morning sun was coming around the summit of the neighboring mountain and it would soon be softening up. We had a few easy runs to begin with, just letting the legs warm up. I could tell they were good skiers straight away, even if a bit awkward on the icy early surface. They were both quick on their feet, made good turns, and seemed used to the icy conditions. I slid out a few times and had to adjust my technique to put more pressure on my edges. By the time I had that sorted the sun was beginning to soften up the snow and we were beginning to ski hard and confidently together. We would ride the series of draglifts back up to the summit after each run. The lift attendants would come out to look at my lift ticket and punch the card but the lads I was skiing with would just give them a wink and a nod and they would go back to their hut. Hamish would ride up with me one lift and Gregor on the other. Both asked me similar questions about the work I was going to be doing out on those islands beyond Oban and the Firth of Lorne. I asked them on different occasions about what kind of work they had been doing. It got me thinking. I would see how the day went skiing. It was going pretty good so far.

Up at the summit amidst the rocks and snow and long-distance views Hamish spoke, wanting to take charge of the run selection.

"I think we're ready for the Flypaper," he said to Gregor who in turn looked at me.

"Aye, right enough. You fit now, Lars?" he asked me.

"I was born ready. Where are we going?"

"Auch, it's just the steepest run in Scotland," Hamish said as he pushed off across the flat plateau and I followed at the rear, just taking in the views and being thankful for the chance to be up here on the summit on such a fine day.

We began a long traverse across a plateau. There was a trail of sorts to follow, packed snow between various sized rocks and boulders, weathered by the wind and covered by lichens. All of the terrain as far as the eye could see seemed devoid of trees. I could see for miles from the snow-covered summits down to the brown slopes with gullies cracked into their hard rocky shells running down to green valleys, these glens of Scotland.

The sun was bright and hot now and the snow was turning soft and slushy. I followed Hamish and Gregor as we worked our way along the summit plateau, passing a few other runs that dropped off and ran down through the rocks and gullies towards the base lodge. I never realized that any of these runs existed from my day in the fog and cloud and rain yesterday. Yesterday I was blind and today I could see. It was all so bright and glorious and I could not believe the difference a day made. We stopped at the edge of a precipice.

"Aye, this'll be the top o' the Flypaper," Hamish said, glancing back at me. Gregor pulled up beside us and just looked out over the Highland scenery. I bent over to buckle my boots tighter for good reason.

"Looks pretty steep," I said, glancing down the long pitch running out onto a flat, almost like an amphitheatre. It reminded me of the outrun from a ski jump, long and smooth and steep.

"She be steep, right enough," Gregor chipped in, adding: "But no moguls. Not many punters come over to ski it."

"I can see why," I said, standing level with them now, having tightened my boots to the extent that they were pinching my feet.

Hamish put his skis out over the edge of the precipice and dropped into the fall line like he had just jumped out of an airplane. Although he was forcing his turns and not showing a lot of style, he managed the steep pitch by literally throwing his body from one turn to the next. He kept turning and somehow recovered from leaning into the hill several times and went out of sight into the steep and then re-emerged as he slid out onto the flat and came to a stop looking back up at us.

"You can go next, Lars," Gregor said to me.

"Snow seems pretty good," I said, trying to boost my confidence.

"Aye, it's soft now, right enough. In a wee while it'll be so soft it will just slide like ball bearings down this pitch."

"Guess we'd best be going then," I said and took a deep breath and lunged myself over the edge. I began to turn, working my skis from one arced turn into another. I drove my knees hard into each turn and found they carved well in the soft snow. It was the first time in a long time I had made proper turns on a straight steep pitch and it felt good. I just remembered to do pole plant turn, pole plant turn, back and forth, just like a pendulum, keeping a low center of gravity throughout. As I continued towards the outrun it stayed steep and I could sense the soft snow now starting to slide with me on each turn. I kept working hard on my turns and soon I saw a sheet of corn snow come sliding past me. Gravity was helping that that snow and I was fighting it with my turns. I just kept turning but it was more like surfing and I rode the wave and felt like I was inventing a new sport. I pulled up alongside Hamish.

"That was something else!" I exclaimed while trying to catch my breath.

"Aye, those were useful turns you made up there, Lars. You've done this before."

"Once or twice. Feels good to be on some steep again," I said in between gulps of air, leaning out over my poles and looking down at the soft corn snow. When I looked up I saw Gregor beginning to make his run down. He was much like Hamish, using his strength to literally muscle his way down the pitch. He looked in control at first but then got steadily faster until the only way out was to lean into the hill. He kissed the snow with his backside but bounded up like a bouncing ball and was into the next turn but had overcompensated and fell over on the other side, but again forced his way back up. He kept going but was now overcome by the wave of sliding snow and just gave up and fell on his side and rode the wave down to where we stood on the flat.

"Aye, it's a wee bit slippery up there, Gregor," Hamish observed.

"Auch, not bad," he replied, standing up and we all laughed together standing in the bright pure sunlight. I liked being on this Scottish mountainside with these guys in early April and felt like I was doing everything right in my life.

"Time for a cup of tea," Hamish said.

"I'll drink to that," I replied.

"Aye, we'll make for the bothy then." Gregor began to push off across the flats towards the lift station and base lodge. I followed and before long we were at the lifts and I was hot, sweaty and thirsty.

A number of people had arrived by now and the place was crowded—just normal people of all ages, out enjoying a Sunday afternoon skiing in springtime. The lift attendants were outside their huts now, checking tickets in the queue. When one of them looked at mine he observed that all of the punches were gone after a hard morning's skiing. Before the attendant could say anything else Hamish had taken him to one side and said a few words. The lift attendant just nodded at me and I smiled back and I presumed I was not going to be bothered the rest of the day.

"Bloody stupid system, right enough," Hamish said after we were gliding up on the draglift.

"Does seem a bit archaic."

"Auch, went out with the Ark, when a copula run was considered a good day."

"Youse guys work pretty hard at your skiing."

"You're not so bad yourself. We'll have a go at some moguls now."

"Sounds good. I suppose that flypaper won't be worth another visit."

"Aye. The sun's right on it. It'll be porridge by now."

"I really liked that run."

"We could tell, right enough."

"It's pretty good skiing with youse guys."

"There's more to come."

The next run found us skiing fast, almost reckless, through the soft snow. At times one had to dodge other skiers on the narrow pistes. Non-stop we went over a headwall between rock outcrops and into a steep mogul field. There was no option but to attack the moguls at full speed, catching air at times, making turns, being reckless, having fun.

People were getting out of our way like a train was going through the piste. A few shouted out words of encouragement; others stood and watched, shaking their heads. In the troughs of the moguls the slushy snow sprayed out like water. On the crest of each bump I tried to turn where the snow was firmer and then plunged into the next trough. Once through the mogul field we traversed across towards a small hut set amongst the rocks and snow and began stripping our gear off. I was breathing heavy and hot but felt like my skiing had reached a new pinnacle.

Hamish said he was going inside to make the tea. Gregor and I sat down on a bench and leaned against the rough stonewall of the hut. I closed my eyes and let the sun's rays just beam down on my face and all over my body. I heard the sounds of other skiers approaching but no voices. The skiers stopped to take their gear off. I wasn't going to bother looking—I just felt good sitting there in the sun, comfortable and happy.

When I opened my eyes I was amazed to see that two young women had joined us.

Both had red hair and freckles, dark eyes and soft lips. They quickly pulled their sweaters off and then undid button-down shirts. Those came off to expose pink-white skin dotted with freckles and black bras covering breasts. All that was left were brown wool plus fours, wool socks and ski boots. They both wore smiles and in a relaxed way introduced themselves to me but said nothing to Gregor. He got up and said he was going to help with the tea.

"You know these guys?" I asked.

"Oh Aye," the one who called herself Helen replied. "They're both local lads. Good lads, aye."

The other one who introduced herself as Fiona looked me straight in the eye and said in her singsong accent, "Wish they spent a wee bit more time here, right enough."

I looked straight back into her dark eyes. "So is this a boyfriend-girlfriend thing?"

"Aye, used to be." They were silent for a while. I decided to keep the conversation going.

"Do you ski here often?"

"When we can, what with shifts and all."

"Auch, it depends on the weather."

"You can say that again," I said to the pair of them, staring at the bare skin and black underwear. They didn't seem to mind. "What a difference a day makes," I concluded.

"Looks like you're enjoying yourself," Helen continued.

"Aye, we saw you coming down with the lads through those bumps," Fiona added.

"You're not bad on those boards, right enough."

"So you decided to follow us down," I stated, trying to keep up with their fast talking.

"Aye. We're all members of the ski club. Or at least our parents are. We get to use this hut."

Hamish and Gregor came out of the bothy, bending their heads to get under the doorframe, carrying steaming mugs of tea, five of them in all. The girls took their mugs and set them down on the bench beside them without saying anything. They both resorted back to the position of eyes closed facing the warm sun. I took the mug offered by Hamish and watched the vapor rising into the clear atmosphere.

"I was just talking to your friends," I said. "Do they always take their clothes off in public?"

"Aye. They're the desperate ones."

"Speak for yourself," one of the girls said, her eyes still closed, soaking up the sun.

The other chipped in with, "Auch, you lot probably didn't even get it as good on yer travels, if you got it at all."

That kept us silent for a while. I sipped my tea and found it too strong and too sweet but I wasn't going to complain, for I was thirsty now. It felt good sitting there.

"It's some place when the sun is shining, eh?" I said after a while. Nobody answered. We just sat there soaking up the sun. Hamish finally spoke.

"Aye, this would be a great place right enough. If only there was just some more work about."

"What do these girls do?"

"Can't you tell?" Hamish replied. "Auch, they're nurses, up in Fort William, at the Belford."

I sat there in the sunshine and thought for a moment and then did it. "Tell me girls, what would you say if I was going to offer jobs to these guys?"

They all sat up and looked at me. Helen seemed to answer for everybody: "We'd havta ask what it was doing, right enough. But then we'd probably ask if there were any jobs goin' for the likes of us, too!" They all laughed, somewhat nervously.

"Auch, I've had enough of bedpans," the other one said in her sweet Scottish voice.

"I'm thinking about putting them to work on a drill rig in Jura," I announced.

"That seems far enough away to me," Helen said while looking straight at Gregor. She cast him a smile. I looked at both of the girls with their white skin and freckles and well supported breasts in black bras.

"Anything that you could do to bring these lads closer to home would be great, aye," Fiona beamed towards Hamish.

"Well, that settles it," I said and had a sip of the tea. It tasted good now and I was thirsty. "We'll drink our tea, then go up and do some more runs before it really turns to that porridge. I'll tell you guys what the job is all about. If you'd like to try it, I'll need you to come down to Oban with me tonight. We have to be on site tomorrow."

"Auch, no need to talk about it Lars," Hamish said and I waited anxiously for him to finish his sentence. "We'll come straight away if you'll have us."

Gregor nodded and the girls smiled and we all looked out at the mountains quietly while we finished our tea.

The Confessional Chairlift

She had been awake for a while, lying naked in the bed. Claudia watched the early morning light creep into the room and listened to Francois, still asleep, breathing slowly and quietly. Carefully she arose, lifting the duvet off her and then tucking it back around the body of her fiancé. Their room at the Club Med was comfortable, albeit a little small and sometimes cool in the morning. This was one of those mornings.

With her arms folded across her chest and palms rubbing her shivering shoulders she walked quickly to the window. Pushing the curtain back a little more gave her a full view of the pistes on this side of La Plagne and the peaks of the Savoie in the distance. Snow groomers were still working on far-away pistes. They looked like ants. Sunlight glistened off their red metal shells. Those piste-bashers were too far away to hear. All she heard was Francois murmuring, perhaps sensing the light. She drew the curtains and marched quickly across the matching pastel green carpet into the toilet, knowing her way in the dark.

The light in the toilet was bright, almost severe the way it reflected off the white ceramic tiles. The same tiles on the floor were cold, sending a shiver up her body. Quickly she laid a towel on the floor and wrapped another around her petite body. Then she looked in the mirror. "*Oui*," she said out loud, thinking to herself how she felt now—still young, still beautiful, still skiing well. But bored. She would take her time and put her makeup on, first brushing the short brown hair and then doing the eyes. No eye shadow, just the brows and lashes today. And nothing else on her face—just plenty of sunscreen. It was going to be sunny today, just like every other day so far this March in the mountains. She dabbed her armpits and splashed a little of the same fragrance of *eau de toilet* on her neck and behind each ear, checking the studs of small diamond earrings at the same time.

There was time for one last look in the mirror. She looked into her brown eyes, pupils dilated in the harsh light. The mirror didn't lie. She looked stunning but not overdone. Those pupils would expand rapidly when she walked back into the dark bedroom. There she dressed in new white underwear and the tight red ski trousers, a blue turtleneck beneath the shoulder straps and a green sweater over the top. Claudia had laid it all out the night before after she told Francois her intention to go skiing. He had encouraged her but was ambivalent to her decision. She found her running shoes and sat on the bed beside Francois, slipping them on, listening to him sleeping. She turned to him, giving him a quiet kiss on the cheek, her body brushing against the hard firmness of the plaster cast beneath the duvet.

She slid her arm beneath the duvet and tapped the plaster. It responded with a hollow sound. She moved her hand up the cold plaster onto the warmth of his abdomen but Francois pushed it away, his eyes still closed. "*Adieu*," she whispered to him, rising from the bed. "*Bon chance*," he said back in a deep quiet voice.

When Lars returned to his room at the Hotel Eldorado she was already gone. He had been to breakfast by himself and felt guilty about not waiting for her. Monica had said she wanted to take a shower, repeatedly resisting his suggestions that they have one together. He had eaten quickly but enjoyed every bit of the buffet, especially the warm flaky croissants smeared with thick creamy butter and topped with strawberry jam. He had stuffed a banana and apple into the pockets of his sweatpants and had deliberately taken another plain croissant and large mug of cappuccino back to the room with him. That was meant to be a surprise for Monica.

He sat on the narrow bed in this single room at the back of the Hotel and sipped the coffee. It tasted bitter and he wouldn't bother to put the tube of sugar he'd brought into it. He dipped the tip of the croissant into the foam at the top of the cup and brought it to his mouth. The croissant didn't taste of anything now, just bits of flaky pastry wetted slightly churning around inside his mouth. That was the same mouth and lips that had been feeling the sensations of Monica's body only minutes before and all through the night. But she was gone now, probably back to her room and her daughter and their friend.

He knew where that room was. She had taken him there last night to give him her business card. He knew the ulterior motive was for the mother to show off the young prize she had attracted before the night's excitements began. The daughter and Monica's friend had been polite and discreet as French women probably were, chatting to Lars in their broken English while she got her things ready. He learned that the daughter was a cabaret dancer in Paris. She looked the type. The friend and the mother ran a travel agency and that was noted on the card he was now staring at alone in the room on a Sunday morning. She would be back in her own room now, probably cuddled up in bed with her daughter, giggling and laughing and gossiping about the fantastic night the mother had with a young American in a narrow bedroom with a narrow bed in the Hotel Eldorado. He felt like he should be in a church, begging for forgiveness. Instead he got ready to go skiing.

He changed out of sweats and into his red ski pants. He fitted the shoulder straps over a t-shirt. It was so warm skiing yesterday afternoon that all he needed was a sweatshirt today and the Michigan Tech one would do. He fitted his US Steel baseball cap over his head and remembered to grab the sunglasses and lift pass and put those around his neck. Then he headed for the basement of the hotel, carrying his ski boots. There were not many sets of skis in the dark concrete walled locker room. His Volkl P9s were the longest ones in the metal rack. With his boots buckled and equipment gathered together, he shuffled along the concrete floor towards the exit. He realized now how stiff, sore, and tired he was. But he was determined to ski it out of him.

The day before had been a full one. He had flown into Heathrow for a Friday morning meeting with the engineering contractor to go through the plant design. They managed to resolve their differences and he put up with the usual excuses about why there were delays and listened to their jokes about his trip just being an excuse to go skiing. The Directors tried to impress him by taking him to a long lunch in their club in Pall Mall. It was well know in the mining industry but he felt out of place in there and kept looking at his watch. Then they put him on a train at Victoria heading for the Channel. He met what the travel agent called the 'ski train' and after the crossing and sorting out his bags in Zebrugge he slept as if he meant it and certainly needed it. It had arrived in the morning and after a coach trip from the station at Aimes to the Belle Plagne village he had time for an afternoon's skiing. But it was not good skiing because he was tired from the traveling and rusty from not having skied since his last trip to Europe.

Things were surprisingly better later in the sauna at the Belle Plagne Health Club. That was where he met Monica, chatted to her, found out she was in the same hotel and asked her to dinner. There was the waiting, the wine, the dinner, and then the decision: Her decision was to spend the night. And now the guilt crept over him like a blanket as he stepped out of the hotel and into the sunlight.

The bright light hurt his eyes. It was still cool and clear in the early morning light but would be hot and sunny later. Snow would turn to slush. That's how it was yesterday and it would be the same today. Presently the snow in front of the hotel was hard from freezing overnight. Lars' skis bounced when they fell onto the hard snow, free from his grasp. Before putting his skis on he did some stretching exercises but that didn't help. He knew it would be a day on the mountain, skiing on autopilot, going through the motions, thinking about it all. With his Ray-Ban sunglasses on and Marker bindings secured and the skis beneath him, part of him now, somehow he felt a little better.

Just before he set off across the hard snow towards a draglift he looked up towards the windows of the Eldorado's dining room. There she was, standing behind the pane of tinted glass, waving at him! She and others in the dining room had been watching him, bending and twisting and preparing for a day's skiing. He only looked at her. Another face moved to the window and waved. He recognized the familiar features of the daughter. It finally occurred to him that he and the daughter were probably the same age. They both blew him a kiss but he failed to notice as he had set off gliding down the slope towards the lift alone, allowing the French women a good morning's worth of gossiping in a mother-daughter sort of way.

He would just have to forget about her and try to have a better day of skiing and tour around the mountain. The snow was pretty hard but he looked towards the East facing slopes where it would be softer in the morning and then he would work his way back as the sun traveled through the sky. It was a good day for being alone and thinking things over and that's what he needed to do after last night's performance with that woman.

Claudia started her day on the piste right adjacent to the Club Med. It was called the Sardonne and had a fast 4-person chair serving it. She put in several hard training-type runs before the crowds came for the lift and the instructors and coaches came out to set courses. The piste was well groomed and already soft in the morning as it faced to the East. As it was so empty she could pick up enough speed and enjoy the morning air, fresh and clear and in her face. Riding up the lift alone she thought back to the days as a teenager when her parents would pack her off from Marseilles in the train and she would come here for weeks of race training. That was before they started the arguing and the fighting and splitting up and the race training stopped because of it. The racing days were over but at least she could still ski well enough to enjoy it. The only thing she didn't enjoy was skiing alone and she gave Francois a thought about how he was faring back at the Club Med. He would be fine and she would be back to see him but she knew things were different already.

When it became crowded she decided to head over to Montalbert. It was at a lower elevation and into the trees. A few rocks were appearing and the slushy snow was difficult to turn in. The sun had gone and a fog had crept up the valley. She did a few more runs and watched couples skiing together and laughing and chatting and enjoying themselves despite the change in the weather. After lunch she continued touring around the mountain, skiing somewhat aimlessly now, not making very good turns, feeling bored with herself at times. This was not a good way for her to ski. She decided she would make her way over to Champagny for the end of the day and force herself to ski better and then be in a better mood to see Francois. She hoped he would be better by then but she also knew it was not easy for him. Things were different.

He saw her standing in the lift line, knowing somehow that she was alone. He could tell by the way she stood confidently on her skis, looking around at everything but focusing on nothing. There were no other singles that he could notice and the queue was large enough to make asking sensible. From behind she had an attractive athletic figure. From the front she was the most attractive young woman he had seen all day, all week, all year. Everything about her was elegant but understated.

"Single?"

"*Pardon*?" came the reply in a heavy French accent. Perhaps this was not such a good idea, Lars thought to himself but pressed ahead anyhow.

"Can you speak English?"

"Of course," came a sweeter, more sympathetic reply this time.

"Then you'll ride up the lift with me?"

"Are you asking or telling?" She beamed back at this good-looking straight-talking American with the nice ass, as they say, and hopefully behind the sunglasses he would not notice she was looking him over.

"I'd say I was asking. You looked like you were skiing alone."

"Yes, I am. Thank you for the invitation."

They immediately began chatting about the nice weather and the nice skiing and where they were from and what they were doing and how long and why here and what sort of work. Somehow they became oblivious to all the other people silently shuffling along on their skis while they got on like a house on fire just making polite conversation; and both wanting to know more already, but then their turn for the lift came and suddenly they were quiet as the chair swept them away and they both took turns looking out at the scenery. Then they looked into each other's eyes for the first time. Sunglasses were off now and eyes were reaching out. The eyes did not lie. For Lars they had gone further than he wanted to. Claudia thought differently. Here was a chance to be different. She would take her chance and ask him.

"Would you care to go skiing with me?"

"Yeah. Why not. We've got time to get a few more runs in before the lifts close."

"Have you tried this 'Hari Kari' yet?" she asked, pointing in the direction that went along a traverse and then down though a steep mogul field back to the other side of the mountain. He didn't look at the scenery. He only looked at her fit body stretching and gesturing.

She noticed that when she turned back to look at him and she gave him a big smile.

"Yeah. I skied it this morning. Moguls were pretty awesome."

"You like skiing le bosses?"

"If that's what you call them."

"You Americans are so direct."

"Not at all like you French women."

She laughed. "What makes you say that?"

"Later. Let's stop the chat and let our skis do the talking. There isn't a lot of time before the lifts close."

"You're right," she said, putting her sunglasses on and hands in pole straps. Lars knew right away she could ski real good and they headed off together for Hari Kari with the afternoon sun descending on La Plange.

Claudia wanted to watch him through the first pitch of moguls. He kept on insisting that it was ladies first, but she made an excuse, gesturing, then bending over as though she wanted to tighten her boots. She watched this American glance down the mogul-infested pitch. He clicked his poles together and set off into the fall line, making quick turns on the steep, controlling his speed. She watched his ass thrust and pump as he came out of the trough of le bosse and drive his knees to turn on the crest and dive into a trough.

"Oui," she said out loud. He was smooth. He skied strong. He would do fine. And he had that nice ass. She giggled a little, thinking about what he might look like naked. Then she realized he had stopped down where the moguls ran out onto a groomed piste. It was her turn.

Lars was breathing heavily after his burst through the moguls. They were still soft even after the sun had gone over the mountain. The shadow was a bit tricky but he had no problem choosing a line and making good turns and he felt better for it. He was having a pretty crummy day up until now with that guilt feeling hanging over him. But now he relaxed and rested on his ski poles as he watched this young French woman tackle the moguls. She was double-pole planting in places, making check turns, nearly coming to a stop but still going—a little shaky in places and leaning back, but recovering and keeping going and then stopping beside him and falling over, chest heaving and gasping for breath.

"*Ah, je n' en peux plus!*" she exclaimed in-between gasps. Lars stood there and watched her, then offered her a hand. She took it and he pulled her up. They both had their sunglasses off because of the flat light. Eyes met and then she looked at the snow sheepishly and then back up at him.

"You skied that very well," she said quietly.

"Thanks. We'd better get a move on. The lift is probably closing in a few minutes."

"*Oui*, it's a straight run from here. You lead, no stopping."

Lars set off; making big fast giant slalom turns down the piste, slushy snow spraying up, skis carving well. He was enjoying his new-found attitude and looked back to see her right behind him, making similar turns, going fast. They passed under the lift line and he noticed there were no people on it. Thinking that this could be trouble, he let the skis run a bit more and the woman followed. Soon they were cruising through the flat run towards the lift station. The attendants were lifting the seats onto the backs of the chairs as they passed. All Lars heard was the sound of metal clanging. He skied right up to the boarding point and the lift attendants ignored him and carried on with their business. The woman came along and began a conversation in rapidly spoken French with the men and they laughed a bit and she laughed back and they pressed a button to open the barriers. She motioned for Lars to come along and soon they were riding up the lift together. The sound of the chairs being prepared for the night recommenced and soon faded away into the distance.

"I didn't think they would let us on the lift."

"There was no difficulty."

"What did you say, if you don't mind me asking?"

"*Oui*—just that you were a poor American boy who had lost his way. I was leading you back to La Plagne and we had a philosophical argument about which way to go."

"I'd hardly say we were arguing."

"*Oui*," she laughed. "A French woman must say she is arguing with a man. It always works."

"What did they say? It must have been funny."

"They wished me well in continuing the argument. This is supposed to be a philosophical chairlift."

Lars shook his head and looked out at the scenery now shrouded in shadow. The sun was ahead of them, still shining on the La Plagne side, but had lost its intensity in the haze and thin cloud moving in. The woman brushed up against him, wanting to get his attention.

"Did you feel like the young American in the movies down there?"

"Sorry, I'm not with you."

"You know, when he is out on the date in the big American Daddy's car with the girl in the pretty dress all innocent and he runs out of what you call it, gas?"

"That's a very interesting description, er..., I didn't get your name. But that scene hadn't entered my mind." All this skiing and talking and he didn't even know her name.

"Claudia." Their eyes met again and they couldn't stop looking at each other.

"Lars. Lars Svensson. I'm glad to meet you, Claudia. Thanks for taking me down this Hari Kari, and for almost getting us stranded."

She laughed. "I am thanking you for choosing me. Tell me, why did you ask me to ride the lift?"

"I dunno. Must have been something between fate and free will."

"Ah, so," she beamed a mouthful of white shiny teeth at him, "you do have some philosophy in you."

"Not really, Claudia. Just high school level. Nothing serious. Are you a philosopher?" The thought crossed his mind that this attractive face and body also had a brain and probably wanted to show it.

"No, of course not. I am selling pharmaceuticals. We're all here at the Club Med for a conference."

"That's the place over by the race training, isn't it?"

"*Oui*. The French National team stays there when training. They used it before the Olympics last month. Everyone says they are still clearing up from the parties."

Lars laughed. "I was in Meribel during the Olympics. Everyone heard the stories about the condom machines down in the Olympic village. They ran out after the first hour."

She laughed as well. "This is true of the Winter Sport in France."

"You can say that again," Lars said as he turned away and looked over at the mogul field they had skied down together. But now all his thoughts were on last night and how that older woman didn't stop even after he had stopped and of all the positions and body movements and he could not remember her name—but she had waved at him and blew him a kiss and he felt so full of guilt again.

He heard the voice urging him to respond.

"I ask again. Will you ski with me tomorrow?" She knew she must ask. They had little time to decide.

"Tomorrow?" Lars shook his head to gather his senses and looked at his watch. The lifts would be closing. He had to be making his way back across the mountain a long way to get to the hotel. Then he looked at her and the eyes reaching out and he knew he would but he should not but the eyes gave it all away.

"Sure. If it's no trouble. I'm here on my own. You probably guessed that anyhow."

"Perhaps. A French woman can tell when a man is interested."

"You don't say."

"Can you come to the Club Med for say nine thirty?"

"That should be enough time. I have to come across from the Eldorado. It's in Belle Plagne."

"Oh, then you have a long ski to return. You must be going."

They were approaching the top of the lift and had to get their things ready and he was concentrating on getting ready to ski and she just watched him.

"Well, I'd better be going. I'll see you tomorrow, nine thirty." He started to set off. He had not said goodbye. She wanted to say goodbye properly and politely but he did not. So she came over to him and thrust her face into his and he awkwardly kissed her and she drew away and looked at him and all he said was, "Bye"—like a taxi driver in New York would say to a pretty woman that would have a conversation during a journey and then never be seen again. He set off and she watched him gliding over the snow on the trail that would lead to the Iversen Tunnel and then back to Belle Plagne.

She took a moment to prepare herself. She stood and looked out over the terrain in front of her. It was the old downhill course, probably not used for years in any major competition. There was still an antiquated timing shack and an official's observation booth clad in oxidized zinc sheets. Something that resembled safety netting followed the curve down at the first turn, a narrow gully that went like a chute and followed a long bend until it was out of sight around a corner. The course was used now by clubs and groups, perhaps a little training by the French team when they stayed here. Her group had paid to use it tomorrow for a mock downhill.

She laughed to herself and thought about the man she had met. He skied like a racer. It would be a joke for either of them to be in a race with her colleagues from work who had never raced before. Claudia's racing days were over with now but she didn't want to embarrass her friends. She really wanted to ski with this American instead. She would find some excuse, talk her way out of it, and perhaps use her concern for Francois. Everybody would know that was a lie. Everything seemed to be a lie. Things were different and she knew it. It was over before they came here on this trip and then he injured his knee trying that snowboarding when he should have stayed skiing with her but now there was this American and she hoped for tomorrow.

But she had to be getting back to Francois now. It would be a night of looking after him, listening to him, stroking his beard, running her hands through his hair. But there could be no lovemaking with Francois. Not now and perhaps not for a long time, maybe never. She would find herself alone and thinking about the man she just met. She was thinking about him now as the late afternoon crept down over La Plagne. Time to be skiing down this old course, making fast turns and feeling the wind in her face one more time. And then tomorrow, yes tomorrow. If only he would keep his promise and come. Perhaps he would not, the way he left her. Perhaps he would, the way he smiled at her. Perhaps, perhaps. Time to ski now, she thought, and set herself over the edge and into the fall line, picking up speed and making a broad sweeping turn towards the chute and the Club Med and Francois.

When Lars opened the door into his narrow hotel room he found an envelope lying on the floor. It had the familiar markings and color pattern of the business card she had given him last night when he was so impatient to be with her and all she wanted to do was show him off. After setting his things down on the bed and taking his sweatshirt off he opened the envelope. It was handwritten, just a few lines on a sheet of matching stationery of the card and the envelope. She had all of these things well organized. Years of practice, Lars thought to himself as he read the words in what he knew would be broken English:

Please to excuse me for this note. I hope you have a good day of Winter sport. I like very much to see you at le sport center where we met In le sauna, if you please. Thank you very much, Monica.

Lars left the note on the small desk beside the bed. There was no mention of time or intention of this meeting but he had a good idea. At least he would not worry about taking a shower. He changed into his sweats and gathered up his toilet bag and a change of clothes and 30FF in loose change to pay for the entry to le sauna.

It was a nice early evening in Belle Plagne, the town streets not very busy, and shops looking vacant. This was the time many of the guests would be getting ready for their dinner. He wondered what Claudia would be doing over at the Club Med now. He also wondered what was happening back home. Maybe he should find a newspaper. He thought of the night before and the night coming and felt the guilt. But he walked on through the mix of dull gray concrete and bright varnished wood frame buildings and continued down concrete stairs until he reached the sports center. He paid to go in and had a quick shower and put the robe on with a towel beneath and headed for the wood-paneled sauna area.

Monica was lying on one of the chaise lounges in the resting room reading a book. Her blonde hair was matted after having been in the sauna. She looked fresher, younger, happier than when he had left her in the bedroom before breakfast. She smiled and pointed to the lounges beside her, acting totally relaxed at first but then setting the book down and standing on her bare feet. She approached him to offer either cheek and he kissed each one, just like he'd seen other French couples do but had never done before, and then he thought that was what Claudia was expecting back up on the mountain as they said goodbye. But now it was hello and how was the skiing and won't you sit down as I have just come from le sauna.

"You look very healthy," he said, smelling her cleanness and fresh-ness as she sat down again. He picked up the skirts of the terrycloth and positioned himself on the lounge beside her.

"Thank you"

"What did you do today?"

"I take my daughter and my friend to the train station."

"Did they have to leave?"

"*Oui.* My daughter, she have what you say, addition? For a new show. My friend, she have to go back to the office."

"Is it just the two of you in the business?"

"*Oui.* It is closed on a Monday so she can travel back."

"What else did you do today?"

"Oh. I go for a walking. Then I sit in the sun and have reading. Later I come here for to have a massage. And now I have you," she emphasized with a big smile and leaned closer to him.

"I need to go in the sauna now. By the way, the word is 'audition.'" He smiled reluctantly at her and then, rising up from the lounge, she stood up to face him. He looked into her gray-green eyes and the lines on her brown red healthy face and her thin neck and small head with the matted hair and he wanted to hug her.

"I have also been thinking about you, all the day."

"So have I, Monica," he said and took the robe off, leaving only the towel covering the rest of his body and she looked him over and put a hand on his hairy chest. But he stepped away and for the first time realized there were other people in this place who were listening to this conversation. He walked into the sauna to take the heat.

He hardly noticed the other people in the large dark wood-lined sauna at first. He just went straight for the water bucket and grabbed the wooden ladle and began spooning out water onto the hot rocks set into the electric sauna stove. The rocks hissed and steamed back at him. It was like an angry conscience to him, listening to the hiss-ing and then feeling the heat. He sat down on one of the upper benches in the darkened room of heat and began to feel the sweat rising out of his body. He looked around at the others already there before him, sweating profusely now, faces reddened, hands wiping sweat off bare skin both male and female. After a few minutes some began to groan and say words under their breath in French and stood up naked to place towels back over their bodies and walk out of the sauna glaring at him. He did not care and went back to the bucket and spooned out the rest of the water. The heat drove everyone else out and with that accomplished he removed the towel, laid it on the bench, and slumped his naked sweating body down on top of it. He closed his eyes and felt the heat and thought about what the hell he was doing.

Minutes passed and he began to feel the sweat rolling off him in huge beads. He could barely stand the heat now himself and wanted to go out. But the door opened and he knew it would be her so he decided he would stay and let her have the moment she wanted with him alone.

"Oh la-la. It is very hot!" she exclaimed after closing the door behind her. She walked towards him and removed the towel covering her body, setting it on the bench beneath him. She then ran her hand smoothly across his chest, wiping the sweat off and bending over to look at him. He opened his eyes for the first time and looked at her.

"I guess I chased everybody out."

"*Oui*, some of them were cursing you as they came out. I was laughing."

"I'll have to learn some French curses."

"I will teach you during our dinner."

"I take it that's an invitation."

"And afterwards?"

"That's up to you, ma'am."

"Then you will come to my room. The bed is, what you say, larger. I have many things to do with you." She touched him again, stroking her hand along the length of his hot sweaty body. She smiled at and said, "I see you are ready now."

He sat up and drew her into him and they kissed and soon their tongues were dancing with each other and he felt all hot and sweaty to her. He felt as if he was going to explode and he wanted her right there. Just then the door opened and two men walked into the sauna and commented in French on the heat. Lars wrapped the towel around him and walked out and she sat down lower to get out of the heat that was making her sweat already.

❊　　　　　❊　　　　　❊

She was clinging to him, all warm and soft and gently sleeping now. He slowly pushed her to one side and climbed out of the bed. She murmured something in French and rolled over, still sleeping but searching for the cover of the duvet. Lars admired her petite lovely body for a moment in the dim morning light and then carefully covered her. He shook his head and then began to search around the room for his clothes.

It was all in a trail across the floor of her room: His trousers, her skirt. Silk stockings scattered amongst the underwear. She had come down to dinner last night late but for good reason. A woman in a tight skirt, high heels and makeup would draw attention anywhere but in a ski resort hotel it was all too much. All eyes in the Eldorado restaurant were on her. The maitr'd directed her to his table where he waited patiently, sipping Pulginy Montrachet. He made sure to greet her in the French style with a kiss on either cheek. They had enjoyed their dinner of oysters followed by peppered steak with a bottle of Château Neuf du Pap and talked together while the rest of the guests watched them, the older woman with the younger man. And then after the restaurant was empty she came over and sat on his lap, revealing the tops of the stockings and the suspender straps for him to touch and her to tease. They spent long moments kissing in the restaurant and then came up to her room and left the clothes all over the floor.

But now he had to be going because he kept his promises and he dressed quickly. He did not have much time to get ready for skiing, let alone clean himself up. Once he was dressed he thought about going to kiss her goodbye but she was sleeping so soundly he just left her and walked out into a darkened corridor and headed for his room.

The snow was once again hard and icy at this time in the morning. The turns that he tried to make were poorly executed on that run down to the first draglift station. He didn't care how he skied right now; he only wanted to be getting over to the Club Med in time for their 9:30 rendezvous as planned. Riding up the first draglift, he tried to think. Think about what he would say to her. Think about what to say when he got home, whenever he got home. But all he could think about right now was last night and all the things they did together. He thought he knew everything. He was wrong and she was so right and showed him the way. The metallic aftertaste of the oysters at dinner reminded him of how they laughed and talked in their broken English. He had brushed his teeth and gargled but still could not take the taste of the dinner and the taste of her off his lips. He reached the top of the draglift and threw the bar at the wire rope acting as a backstop and then began to ski across to towards her side of the mountain.

Claudia felt like she had all the time in the world that morning. She had risen early, wanting to start it all over again, and had been down to breakfast just as the GA's were setting up the buffet and arranging things for the day. They all chatted to her and asked her how her boyfriend was and she told them he was recovering but she would bring him breakfast and they said to help herself. They also asked what she would be doing for skiing this fine day and she said she had made arrangements and winked at one of the good looking men and he understood immediately. She had a cup of coffee while continuing to flirt with these Frenchmen and then filled up a tray full of food. It would be enough to provide Francois with a nice breakfast and the American man a lunch out on the mountain later. She was certain this American would like that and she would eat it herself if he didn't rendezvous.

She could hear his deep American accented voice before she saw him through the crowd of guests putting their skis on in the bright light outside the complex. All of her colleagues were there and they were laughing and chatting and getting ready for another morning of lessons before their long lunch.

"Sorry lady, I don't work here," she heard him say to the plump area manager from Manchester. She already had enough of this Englishwoman and her drinking games.

"Oh, but you look just like one of the instructors."

"Honest lady, I'm here to meet somebody," he said and saw Claudia coming towards him looking completely beautiful in the same tight red ski pants. He clomped through the crowd over the now snow for it had warmed up already. They kissed in the French style on each cheek and didn't say anything other than "*Bonjour*" to each other and he helped her carry the skis over to where his were lying in the snow. The comments came in French and Dutch and English.

"Must be a guide."

"How did you manage to organize that, Claudia?"

"Can I have him tomorrow?"

Claudia by now had her skis on, ignoring the banter and smiling at Lars all the time. He smiled at the group and knew what they were thinking but would let her do the talking. She said a few words in French which made the men in the group laugh. Then she spoke in English to the plump woman: "This is Lars. We have agreed to be skiing together this day. Perhaps I see you all later. Enjoy your lesson and the race."

"Looks like you'll be enjoying yours, Claudia," the plump woman said to their backs as the couple in the matching red ski pants pushed off together across the flat pitch. Everyone watched as they made good turns side by side heading down the piste towards the Sardonne lift and comments were made about "how lucky she was to find such a good skier and what would Francois think and do today and Francois could take care of himself and so could Claudia and we'd better be starting our lesson and where should we have lunch today and I need to get the edge off this hangover."

There was no queue at that time in the morning and they got straight on the lift and passed over the top of the finish area for the ski stadium. The pitch was well groomed and instructors were already out setting courses starting at a headwall about halfway up the long pitch of the Sardonne piste. She had taken her gloves off and had lifted her sunglasses onto her forehead.

"So, where would you wish to be skiing?"

"Gosh Claudia, I dunno. This pitch here looks pretty good. Maybe we ought to take a run down it before they close it for the race."

"I do not think it is for the race yet. Perhaps they are training or instructing. But yes, it would be good to loosen up here."

"Yeah," Lars said, reading from the piste plan. "We can go from there over to Champagny and get on the other side by the Sud Vernon chairlift."

"And then perhaps we go to ski this Hari-Kari again?"

"Is that just so that we can discuss philosophy again?"

"Oh, then you understood what I said to my colleagues! I told them we were going off to discuss philosophy."

"Not again, Claudia. Besides, this ain't the philosophical chairlift."

"Oh, but to a Frenchwoman everything is philosophical. You see, was it fate or free will which made you decide to come skiing with me today? And the choosing of the color of your ski pants to match those of mine. Those are the questions."

"I think you're putting too much into it for this time in the morning, Claudia. I came skiing because you asked and I had nothing better to do. And these are the only pair of ski pants I've got."

She laughed at him and punched him on the shoulder and he laughed with her and then looked at her in the eyes and they looked for a long time; but he didn't want to go any further, at least not yet, and decided to discuss her colleagues back at the Club Med instead. She told him more about her work and the other people who had come to be together and discuss their new line of products. She said how she had wanted to be a doctor but never made it and this was the next best thing and besides she nearly made as much money as a doctor. She had told her boss she had met someone who was a good skier and would like to go with him today rather than stay with the group that was slow and boring. Her boss had told her she was lucky to meet a good skier who was also good looking and Lars couldn't believe she was saying all this.

"So that must make me fast and exciting?" he asked when she was finished.

"*Oui*," she replied and leaned towards him as if to kiss him; but he turned away to look down the long groomed piste where the course was being set.

"We're almost at the top. We'll go straight at it. I'll lead. That'll be fast and exciting."

"*Oui*," she said again quietly and began getting her things ready and they lifted the safety bar and slid off the lift on soft slushy snow and dodged barriers to come to the top of the course. A sign with words "Course Privet" was firmly planted in what would be the starting gate. Lars clicked his poles together and looked back at Claudia who was just behind him, cruising along and steady on her skis.

"Top to bottom non-stop, eh?" he said back to her and she nodded and smiled and he put his skis into the fall line.

With his skis running fast and making turns he could forget about everything. The wind was in his face and it felt warm. The sun was bright and reflecting off the snow. His skis were turning well and he was making broad sweeping fast turns once past the men setting the course who stopped their work to watch the pair of them cruising past at high speed. The pitch became steeper and Lars adjusted his stance to compensate, still making fast smooth turns. The snow beneath him was perfect, the hardness having just gone before the sun would turn it all slushy.

The fist headwall came at him and he set himself up to make a turn right at the crest and he unweighted enough to pre-jump and caught a little air but stayed in control. By now his breathing was heavier and his legs began to ache a little but he was going fast and he knew Claudia was behind him a few turns back. The last headwall approached before the final steep pitch to the finish and he now had tired legs and didn't prejump as well and caught more air. He was going too fast for the finish and people were wandering around on foot in the finish area and he had to press down hard and try to stop and nearly collided with someone who was shouting at him in French. He sprayed up a big rooster tail of slushy snow in the finish area and bent over to catch his breath.

He looked for Claudia who had cut around the finish area and was bent over with her chest heaving. He watched her and hardly heard the shouts at him in French, and then he saw she was laughing at him as he tried to say "pardon, pardon" and followed their gestures to get out of the finish area and joined Claudia. They laughed together while still trying to catch their breath and she looked beautiful to him.

She shouted back at the race officials and she put her arm over Lars who was bent over still trying to catch his breath. The officials just laughed and waved their arms and went back to their business. She stood straight and closed her eyes and took in deep breaths just like her coach had told her years ago. It was fun to be doing that all over again, skiing fast, having fun. Only this time it was with a man and she was a woman now and not a girl. She enjoyed chasing him at high speed down the mountain and over the headwalls and into the finish just like in a big race. She enjoyed watching his buttocks flex again with each turn he made, pushing hard into the turn and then flexing the buttocks to unweight and begin another turn. She was close to him and heard him breathing and opened her eyes to look at the curve of his behind. Something came over her and she reached over and patted his buttocks gently and spoke softly.

"That was a very nice ski. We do that very well."

"Thanks," he said standing straight now and looking directly at her. "Let's head up that other lift now and get over to Champagny."

She hoped he would say something else or embrace her but maybe it was too early so she dutifully followed him along what was an older chairlift. It was running slow but would take them to where it would be less crowded. There was no queue for this lift and they found themselves together with glasses off now in a cozy old two-seater but didn't say anything to each other.

He was thinking about the night before and the way that woman kept saying *oh-la-la* before she screamed and the way she kept going even after he had stopped and could go on no longer but then got more out of him; and now he was riding this chairlift and going skiing with another beautiful Frenchwoman and he didn't know what to say to her.

Claudia was thinking about Francois being alone back in the room and the harsh words they had spoken last night and how he had said he was only there for the sex but now they couldn't even do that and it would be months and she said she wanted love and passion but he said there was never any of that and they argued about spending the rest of this life together. She had wanted to make it all up with him this morning with the nice breakfast, but he said there was no use in staying so he was going to organize the train to take him back to Paris. She could stay if she wanted, he said, and she felt guilt about wanting to go skiing with this American man who was a good skier and she had not skied like that so fast in years. She had told him to suit himself, but she would deal with the luggage and she said she would see him back at the Apartment in La Defense; and he said perhaps—and that was the last word he spoke. The she spoke to Lars:

"I did not like the way you kissed me goodbye yesterday."

He turned to look at her and their eyes met and drilled into each other. Lars took his time to answer.

"Sorry. I had a lot on my mind."

"What is the problem? Do you not like me?"

"We've only just met."

"That does not matter. Do you not find me attractive?"

"Claudia, you are the most beautiful woman…"

"Then what is the problem?"

"I'll tell you what the problem is. I just left a woman, an older woman though a very attractive and demanding woman, back at my hotel."

"She is your wife? Are you guilty to be talking to me?"

"No, my wife is back in the States. I met this one in La Plagne."

"Do you have feeling for her?"

"Yes, but the wrong type."

"Then what is the problem with me?"

"There is no problem with you. Are you interested in me?"

"Yes, of course."

"Then you want to go to bed with me? Isn't that how all French-women think?"

"Perhaps," she shrugged and leaned closer to him and then plunged her face into his. Their lips touched and parted and hot tongues danced together and bodies melted into each other and their lips and tongues were warm and moist and sensitive to each other and they explored and found what they wanted and withdrew.

"That was a nice kiss," she said and was now firmly beside him, looking at him and their eyes did not look anywhere else with mountains all around them. They didn't say anything to each other for a long time after that. She just followed him.

They skied together the rest of the morning, making their way across the mountain and enjoying the pistes. Every time they went up a chairlift or even when riding a draglift to connect between chairlifts or pistes they would make attempts to kiss each other. When the kissing stopped they began speaking to each other again. She started by pointing out the features of the mountain scenery to him. From the Roch di Mio they could see across to *le tre vallees*, the slopes of Courcheval clearly visible cutting through the trees. Lars had told her of his exploits there during the Olympics, skiing deep powder in the couloirs, drinking in the bars, and watching the women's downhill. She asked him if he tried to attract any of the female competitors. He said no to that as he had his wife with him on that trip. She asked why and if anything was different now and he said lots of things were different now but the most different thing was meeting her. Claudia suggested they ski over to the summit at di Mio and have some lunch.

The restaurant there was crowded so they left their skis in racks and went in to use the toilets. Lars took a long look at himself in the mirror of the basement toilet. His face was well tanned following his skiing a month ago and now he was back again, becoming more tanned. He hadn't the time to shave that morning and looked rugged. The moments of a long night with Monica seemed a long time ago now. The moments with his wife he could barely remember. But soon the season would be over and he would be back trying to resurrect the love and nothing would change. But for now he was skiing with this woman and she was skiing good and even kissing him better and they were enjoying each other's company and he shook his head and wondered where it would lead; and he climbed back up noisy concrete steps and saw her waiting in a queue at the bar.

"You wish to have a *bier*?" she asked when he approached and she gestured to take him in her arms.

"I'll get these, Claudia. What would you like?"

"No, you are the guest. I have even brought you some food. Please, wait outside and we will find a quiet place in the sun."

"Sounds good to me. I hate crowds. Even worse, I hate the prices in these mountain restaurants."

"Then we are the same. I see you outside."

Lars went back out into the sunshine and found a spot to stand where she could see him on the way out of the bar. He took a moment to look at all the other people milling around. They were all in their brightly colored ski apparel. Some were taking skis off; others putting them back on again. Groups were trudging through the slushy snow, chatting to each other in French, lighting up cigarettes, and laughing. Another day at the top of Europe and everybody seemed to be enjoying their holiday. He looked out at the mountains now and looked at the Bellecote Glacier and the view reminded him of Summit County. He was thinking about his skiing there and the powder and the women he met but never knew when he felt the cool, then cold sensation on the back of his neck. He jumped and waved his arms and nearly knocked the beers from her grasp.

"You startled me!"

"*Oui*," she said with that sly smile. "You were looking and thinking far away from here."

"Got that right. Where should we go?"

"Why not over there?" she asked quietly, pointing in the direction he had been looking. There was a long flat field of snow beyond the connecting trails and he nodded, as there were no people. He took one of the bottles of beer from her and set off.

"We almost ought to ski over there."

"We can if you prefer," she replied, stopping as if to turn back and get the skis.

"No, we'll walk. It gives me a chance to look at you walking. Cheers," he said finally and had a sip of the beer and it tasted cool and sweet and fine.

"*Sante*," she said and had a quick sip herself and set off again and he watched her playfully for a moment and then set off to catch up to her.

"You walk nicely."

"In ski boots? You must be joking."

"Well, this isn't exactly the Champs Elysee."

"If I was on the Champs Elysee you would be seeing me in high heels, stockings and a short skirt. Perhaps a white blouse and sunglasses, no?"

"Yeah, I could picture you like that. But this is La Plagne, we're on the top of a mountain, and you look beautiful." He had forgotten everything he had been thinking about.

"I thank you for the compliment. But you really should be seeing me in something other than these skiing clothes."

"Perhaps later?"

"Perhaps."

"You like saying that word."

"It is what a Frenchwoman always says. But now I say we have some lunch. I have brought you something."

"This is awfully nice of you, Claudia."

"Why don't we stop here," she said as they reached the edge of the slope. The crowds were behind them back at the restaurant and the only thing in front of them was an empty white slope and in the distance the range of mountains with peaks towering high and pistes cut through the trees and the town in the bottom of the valley shrouded in haze. She handed Lars her bottle of beer. He set both of them down together in the snow. Claudia took the jacket off from over her shoulder and was pulling objects wrapped in napkins from the pockets. Then she lay the jacket down on the snow and gestured to him.

"Now we are ready for dining. Please to have a seat."

"Thank you," he said. "I can't believe this is happening!" And he approached her and put his arms around her and began kissing her;

but she had the sandwiches in her hands and stepped back from him. She gestured again to the jacket lying on the snow.

He sat down first and made sure he had left enough room for her to have a spot on the jacket. She handed him both of the sandwiches and then she pulled her sweater off over her head and he sat there looking at her body in tight ski trousers like sand flowing through an hourglass. She set the sweater down as additional protection from the snow and sat down beside him. Their bodies were touching and she felt warm to him and just looked so beautiful, being with him up here in the mountains.

He handed her back one of the sandwiches and began to unwrap his. It was a piece of French bread, sliced, with what looked like brie cheese stuffed in the middle and oozing out the sides. The bread still smelled fresh and he took a bite and it was first the hard bread on the roof of his mouth and then the soft creamy cheese and he could also taste fresh butter. On the next bite he also tasted something sweet. She had sliced grapes and they were also in the sandwich. It tasted so good and he was so hungry that he wanted to eat all of it right then but he stopped to talk to her.

"This is fantastic, Claudia."

"Thank you," she said, shrugging her shoulders and giving him a smile, just finishing a bite herself.

Lars took a swig of his beer and looked out at the mountains. There was nobody else in sight ahead of where they sat, just the mountains.

"How did you get these?"

"I made them myself, from the buffet at breakfast."

"No problem smuggling them out?"

"No problem."

"Then you were certain I was going to show up."

"*Oui*, I knew you would be coming. A Frenchwoman knows these things."

"And I suppose a Frenchwoman knows what I want to do later. Will you be able to smuggle me back into the Club Med?"

"Perhaps."

"There's that word again."

She looked him in the eyes again and gave him a smile and before he brought his face into hers she had a bite of her sandwich and looked away. He went back to his eating and finished his sandwich and really wanted more. He seemed to want more of everything right now. He looked out at the mountains and sipped his beer and she finished her sandwich and began to position herself to lie down on the snow with the coat and sweater beneath her and soon he was on top of her. Her mouth tasted of the brie cheese at first and then the warmth and wetness overcame it and they were both overcome by each other and wrestled each other until they were comfortable together, kissing and touching and feeling and lying together in the snow and they were both excited and didn't want to stop but had to as it had to end sometime.

Claudia mumbled something in French which sounded to Lars like "*Je voudrois tu*" and he knew she wanted him and had her eyes closed and now opened them and the first thing she looked into were his bright blue eyes set against the backdrop of the perfect blue sky and everything was wonderful and wet and warm now for her.

"That was another nice kiss. I thank you."

"Thanks for lunch. Would you like to do some more skiing?"

"That would be very nice, but do we need to? We are doing everything nice together."

"I know. I only wish it could last longer." He moved closer again to kiss her softly on the lips once more, then stood up and offered her a hand. "C'mon Claudia, let's go skiing." He helped her up and they embraced once more and he squeezed and rubbed and touched everything he could while they kissed and tongues darted in and out again and then the knew they had to stop. He picked up her sweater and then her coat.

"The sweater is still dry but I'm afraid the coat is a little wet."

"It does not matter. Other parts of me are wet, too. But I am happy for that," she said with a sly smile and gently rubbed him, and said, "We must take care of that."

"Perhaps later?"

"Now you are using that word! Come, we must ski," she said, patting him on the buttocks and then grasping his hand to lead him back towards the restaurant where all the people and their skis were waiting. They didn't notice the other people and went back to their skiing.

Lars felt renewed energy and vigor in his skiing. It was almost as though his skis were weightless, an extension of his body. He had not had that feeling in a long time. He led Claudia to all parts of the mountain, taking the pistes non-stop except in sections were there were fields of moguls. He would stop after attacking a steep mogul field and look up to watch her making aggressive attempts through the bumps. She was keeping up well and trying her best and he could see she was winded after each pitch through the moguls but would then catch her breath on the cruising sections. Their tour around the mountain found them back at the old two-seater chairlift. After embracing and kissing for a long while she withdrew and looked away as though she needed time. He left her to sit and think as the lift chugged away up the mountain, pulleys on lift towers squeaking as their chair passed.

Claudia thought about skiing with this man and while kissing him was thinking about her boyfriend and his struggle to get back on the train and wondering if she would see him again and how he would manage and what would he say about all this.

"I have a boyfriend, too."

"I could have figured that."

"He is very nice to me."

"That's what they all say."

"We have, what you say, 'open relationship.'"

"Is that why you're so keen on me? And don't say 'perhaps'?"

She looked him in the eyes again and smiled and then laughed to herself. She looked out at the mountains and then looked back at him.

"You know what he says sometimes after visiting? 'I'm only here for the sex.'"

"Looking at you I'd say you were well equipped for that," Lars replied and cast a glance up and down her body and then stroked his hand on her thigh.

"Oh Lars, I want more than that. I want passion. I want meaning. I want love."

"That's a lot to ask for. You're making some confession, Claudia."

"But this is the confessional chairlift. You confessed to me this morning."

"You're right," Lars said. "Let's start on the passion." And he launched his face into hers and started on a kiss, and warm moist lips touched again and soon tongues were entwined together under a bright sun. They both made certain the other knew that each other wanted more. Lars pulled away to look at her, desire all though his body. She looked him over and touched him with her hand, gently. She was on fire.

"We need to do more. Should we go somewhere?"

"*Oui*, back to the philosophical chairlift. I wish to ski those moguls again."

"Oh, so its back to the skiing again."

"This is what we came here for."

By late afternoon Claudia had decided they had done as much as possible to that mountain. Skiing le bosses until their legs ached and hearts were pounding was worth it. After skiing down the mogul-infested pitch at les Crozats this man had said it was even better than sex. She presumed he was joking and kissed him passionately and pictured him working his way through le bosses so smoothly and quickly. And then racing down the groomed pistes with the wind in their face and going fast and having fun and just being alive! Claudia had never enjoyed a day so much in her life. She felt so warm and contented and tingly all over and it was time to thank him. Presently they were riding the philosophical chairlift after having made an exhilarating run down Kamikaze. There was a Dutch gentleman on the lift with them. Lars was discussing the meaning of life while the Dutchman smoked a pipe, the aroma of tobacco filling the air. They could have been in a pub in Amsterdam. This gave her an idea. She gently elbowed him and pointed to the restaurant by le Grand Rochette.

"Please, I wish to buy you a beer now," she whispered.

Lars turned from his conversation. "Sounds like a good idea to me, Claudia. I'm pretty thirsty."

"We have been skiing very hard."

"I haven't skied this hard in years. It's been great."

"For me, the same feeling, and more. Do you wish to ski like this again tomorrow?"

"If that's okay with you. It's what happens tonight." He raised an eyebrow and attempting to look into her eyes. She met him head on.

"Please, we have the beer and then we talk."

"Is this more philosophy? Fate and free will over beer?"

"No more philosophy," she said with a smile to Lars and then looked across to the Dutchman. "This lift is nearly complete. It is not everyday that one decides on the meaning of life, no? We bid you good day."

The Dutchman smiled at them while putting his pipe away and gathered up his things. "*Bonjour, mademoiselle*," he said politely. "I bid you both farewell and good luck in this life, whatever the meaning. I think you will have more discussions on this."

"You can say that again," Lars replied and then turned to look at Claudia straight in the eyes while lifting the safety bar to depart the philosophical chairlift.

While he was enjoying the sweet grainy taste of a Kronenborg, Claudia surveyed the scene from the balcony. It looked out over the starting hut for the old Downhill course running down to La Plagne Centre. Beside the shed was that observation building, fitted with windows and sheets of galvanized metal, snow piled high on its flat metal roof. The metal had long lost its luster. It must have been used long ago by officials and maybe even television commentators for the big races and then by crowds. Those were races she never saw, even though she so much wanted to as a little girl. And now she was a woman and it was all over for the racing but not over for her. Especially not now. She watched the telecabine cars coming up and going down the mountain. The cars were empty and the deck was deserted now, everyone making their way off the mountain. It was her time.

"Have you finished?" she asked Lars.

"Yeah, thanks a lot. That hit the spot."

"Do you feel good?"

"I feel great."

"Follow me then. I want to look at something."

"Just looking at you is enough for me."

She stood up and walked off the balcony, ski boots clomping on the wood. He followed and caught up to her as she was marching across slushy snow towards the starting shed.

"What's up," he asked.

"You'll see," she replied and reached for his hand and they walked together and looked out at the hazy sun hovering above the ridgeline of majestic mountains. The sun was making its way down across the valley but was still delivering warmth. Claudia felt warm all over her body now, tingling so much that she was weak at the knees. Both of the small buildings were on stilts and they walked up the snow-covered ramp into the starting hut. There was snow on the floor and they were looking over the staring gate. The electric timing equipment had been removed and they inspected the place where the racer would place his poles over the starting wand and into holes in the snow before launching off down the ramp and into the first turn.

"My colleagues were having a race here today."

"Looks like you missed it."

"I did something better."

"I'm glad."

"You never told me about your racing."

"How did you know I raced."

"A woman can tell these things."

"That was in the past. What else can a woman tell?"

"When she is happy to meet a man, and he is happy to be with her," she said softly and stepped up to him and began kissing intensely.

Once they were in the embrace she stepped back until they were propped up against the wall of the starting hut and they were out of the sun and in the shadow and kissing each other and the passion was rising and she knew it was time. She pulled away and led him by the hand out of the starting hut and across the slushy snow to the metal-clad observation building. Their ski boots clomped on the metal stairs and when she tried the door it was open as she expected it would be. The room was vacant but warm and well lit from the windows, late afternoon sun streaming in and feeling pleasant. There was a long wood shelf running at an angle down from the windowsill along the length of the room. It would have served as a desk for the papers of officials or media watching an important race in days gone by. Claudia looked out at the course and thought about all the racing she missed and all the love and passion she seemed to miss now, too, and felt like it was her time to change things in this warm vacant room overlooking the race course. She set her things down on the desk and looked at Lars.

"You have no hurry to go back to Belle Plagne, no?" she asked.

"No. Time is on our side." He took her into his arms.

"Then we will have our time here. Our time for passion."

"Wouldn't you rather go back to the hotel? I mean, I can get a taxi back and…"

She interrupted him by putting a finger gently on his lips. She hugged him and looked over his shoulder down the piste and over at the gondolas coming up and going down the telecabine and spoke to the window: "No, I am wanting this now." She stepped out of the embrace and looked him in the eyes.

"You know this will be awkward," he said.

"We don't know until we try."

He shrugged his shoulders and smiled and nodded and made all the right gestures and made her feel comfortable like he meant it and it wasn't going to be cheap or dirty but rather a new sign of their passion. Excitement flooded through both of them as they began undressing each other, still kissing and touching. Before long they were undressed as far as they could go and had laid their clothes on the floor and stood looking at each other, hands gently caressing each other's chests.

"It would be nicer for you if I was in high heels, dress and stockings, no?"

He laughed. "Ski boots will have to do." Then he bent down to unbuckle her Nordicas and he unbuckled his Langes and they helped each other with the matching red ski pants and then the underwear. The lovemaking, on the floor of the building, was fantastic for both of them and seemed like it was never going to stop. Neither one of them wanted it to stop but it did stop and then they helped each other dress again. There was nothing bad and they felt good and continued to kiss and look at each other. When they walked out of the building and back down the metal steps a voice shouted at them from the restaurant. It was a pisteur, holding up one bright green ski and one blue ski belonging to each other. Claudia shouted back in French and the pisteur laughed and set the skis back.

"More philosophy, right?" Lars asked as they walked back up to the restaurant through the slushy snow holding hands.

"No, this time it was a confession."

"What sort of confession?"

"The sort of confession a woman makes when she wants to see a man again."

"So I guess that means we'll be skiing together tomorrow?"

"*Oui*, if that is what you wish."

"What I really wish is to spend the night with you."

"You know that would not be possible. No, not tonight."

"Not even a perhaps?"

She smiled at him as they were getting their skis ready and stepping into bindings. She kissed him and finally replied, "Perhaps, no. Tomorrow is another day and I very much look forward to your company. Until then..." She gave him another kiss and then turned on her skis and went off in the direction of her hotel. She skied with style and Lars watched her on the empty piste until she was out of sight. He felt happy and did not follow her.

Claudia found a note in her now empty room along with his suitcase packed up for her to take back to Paris. There was also a message from her boss to remind her to bring down the papers for the meeting and join him for a drink and tell him about her skiing day with the good American. That was to be at 7 p.m. so she didn't have much time to get ready, but she would be ready and she could use a drink.

When Lars came back to his room there was another note on the familiar stationery waiting for him. He opened the envelope and read about her thanking him and saying she was leaving but "please to travel to Paris someday" to see her; she appended her private telephone number with two digits between each hyphen, like the French did.

He crumpled the note and took a shower and then spent that quiet time before going down to dinner alone, lying on his bed and thinking about skiing tomorrow.

About the Author

Kurt Larson comes from the backwoods of Michigan where he was raised from his birth there in 1958. While studying Mining Engineering at Michigan Technical University he earned beer money by writing for the *Michigan Tech Lode*, Houghton's *Daily Mining Gazette* and occasionally *Ski Racing* magazine. Kurt believed in not letting schooling get in the way of his education and as an engineer in training did a lot of skiing across North America. One night in a bar he was asked to take up a job as a Mining Engineer in the United Kingdom. Kurt looked at it as an excuse to ski in Europe. Now his day job is Director of a company in the minerals industry. He also does regular contributions to *Skillings Mining Review* and writes the occasional technical paper. Kurt Larson is grateful for the time he has with his family living between the mountains and the sea in Lochaber on the west coast of Scotland.

0-595-23618-9

Printed in the United Kingdom
by Lightning Source UK Ltd.
1767